Seven-year-old Tara adored Phoebe Grant and decided she wanted her as a nanny. And whatever his daughter wants Dominic Ashton bought her. The demure Miss Grant had taken some persuading but she'd turned out to be perfect in her new role—too bad she'd only agreed to stay until the New Year...

But Phoebe had her reasons—if Dominic Ashton had forgotten their first meeting years before, she certainly hadn't. And she couldn't help but wonder what would happen when Dominic discovered he was employing a woman he'd once branded a tramp—a woman he'd thrown out of his home and his bed!

Dear Reader

Welcome to the latest title in our compelling series: NANNY WANTED!, in which some of our most popular authors create nannies whose talents extend way beyond taking care of the kids! This month we have a special yuletide story to thrill you from bestselling author Sara Craven! And, as Dominic Ashton and his seven-year-old daughter are about to discover, some nannies aren't just for Christmas they're for life!

Wishing you all the joys of the season and happy reading throughout the New Year.

The Editors

Sara Craven started writing for Mills & Boon in 1975 and has since sold over 17 million copies of her books throughout the world. Apart from writing, her passions include films, music, cooking and eating in good restaurants. She now lives in Somerset and is a veteran of many television quiz shows including *Fifteen to One* and *Mastermind*.

A NANNY FOR CHRISTMAS

BY
SARA CRAVEN

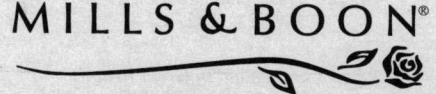

DID YOU PURCHASE THIS BOOK WITHOUT A COVER?

If you did, you should be aware it is **stolen property** as it was reported *unsold and destroyed* by a retailer. Neither the author nor the publisher has received any payment for this book.

All the characters in this book have no existence outside the imagination of the author, and have no relation whatsoever to anyone bearing the same name or names. They are not even distantly inspired by any individual known or unknown to the author, and all the incidents are pure invention.

All Rights Reserved including the right of reproduction in whole or in part in any form. This edition is published by arrangement with Harlequin Enterprises II B.V. The text of this publication or any part thereof may not be reproduced or transmitted in any form or by any means, electronic or mechanical, including photocopying, recording, storage in an information retrieval system, or otherwise, without the written permission of the publisher.

This book is sold subject to the condition that it shall not, by way of trade or otherwise, be lent, resold, hired out or otherwise circulated without the prior consent of the publisher in any form of binding or cover other than that in which it is published and without a similar condition including this condition being imposed on the subsequent purchaser.

MILLS & BOON and MILLS & BOON with the Rose Device are registered trademarks of the publisher.

*First published in Great Britain 1997
Harlequin Mills & Boon Limited,
Eton House, 18-24 Paradise Road, Richmond, Surrey TW9 1SR*

© Sara Craven 1997

ISBN 0 263 80480 1

*Set in Times Roman 10½ on 11 pt.
01-9712-52421 C1*

*Printed and bound in Great Britain
by Mackays of Chatham PLC, Chatham*

CHAPTER ONE

'YOUR favourite customer is back.' Lynn shouldered her way through the swing doors into the kitchen with a tray of dirty crockery.

'That little girl again?' Phoebe glanced up, frowning, from her task of adding a salad garnish to a plate of egg mayonnaise sandwiches. 'Is she still on her own?'

'As ever was.' Lynn began expertly to pack the dishwasher. 'Odd, isn't it?'

Phoebe's frown deepened. 'I think it's downright irresponsible of someone,' she said roundly. 'She's far too young to be wandering around the streets alone. I wouldn't say she was much more than seven.'

'She's safe enough in here,' Lynn pointed out fairly. 'The Clover Tea Rooms isn't exactly a meeting place for kidnappers and perverts.'

'As far as we know,' Phoebe said grimly, filling a milk jug and placing it on her own tray together with a teapot, a sugar basin and the sandwiches.

As she carried it through to the dining room she cast a worried glance towards the corner table by the window and its small occupant.

The child had been coming in for the past three days, at the same time each afternoon. On the first occasion Phoebe had assumed she was waiting for some adult to join her.

Instead, the little girl had asked for a menu.

'Would you like me to tell you what there is?' Phoebe had suggested, receiving a look of utmost scorn for her pains.

'I can read it for myself, thank you,' a clear, remarkably self-possessed voice told her, before placing an order for a sultana scone and a cup of hot chocolate.

Even then, Phoebe hesitated. 'Wouldn't it be better to wait for the rest of your family? Our food is quite expensive, you see.'

Scorn deepened into outrage in the child's eyes. 'I can afford to pay,' she announced with immense dignity. She delved into her tote bag and produced a crisp five-pound note. 'Will that be enough?'

'More than enough,' Phoebe allowed evenly, and went to get the order.

Her meal finished, the little girl paid, worked out a tip with frowning concentration and left. A pattern that had now become established, although it made Phoebe no happier.

This time, the child asked for hot milk with honey and nutmeg and some home-made biscuits.

'You're becoming quite a regular,' Phoebe remarked, trying to sound casual as she placed the order on the table. 'But, unlike most of our customers, we don't know your name.'

There was a pause, then the little girl said doubtfully, 'I'm not supposed to talk to strangers.'

'And quite right too,' Phoebe approved warmly. 'But I'm hardly a stranger. For one thing I feed you every day, and, for another, my name's pinned on my shirt. So...?' She waited expectantly.

There was a pause, then the child said reluctantly, 'I'm Tara Vane.'

'That's a pretty name.' Phoebe gave her an encouraging smile. 'Do you live in Westcombe?'

This brought a decisive shake of the head. 'I live at Fitton Magna.'

Phoebe was silent for a moment, angry to realise that her heart was pounding suddenly. It's only a place, she reminded herself. And what happened was six years ago. It has nothing to do with here and now.

'I see,' she said slowly. 'Then you have a long journey home.'

Tara gave her a superior look. 'It's fifteen miles. It doesn't take long in the car.'

'Ah.' Phoebe relaxed with an effort. 'Then you go home with Mummy.'

She saw the small back stiffen. 'I haven't got a mummy. Not any more.'

Oh, God, Phoebe groaned inwardly. She said quietly, 'I'm very sorry, Tara. It—it's something we have in common, I'm afraid.'

Tara gave her an interested look. 'Then do you live with your daddy too?'

Phoebe bit her lip as the pain of all too recent events slashed at her again. 'No, I'm afraid not.'

'I expect he's away on business,' Tara said thoughtfully. 'My daddy's away all the time. That's why I have Cindy to look after me.'

Oh, do you? thought Phoebe. Then she's not making a very good job of it.

Aloud, she said gently, 'Everyone needs someone, Tara. And it's good that we've got to know each other a little. Now we can say hello if we meet in the street.'

'I'm not in the street very often.' Tara sipped her milk. 'When I finish school, I have my piano lesson and then I come here and wait for Cindy.'

'Found out all you wanted to know?' Lynn asked with amusement when Phoebe returned to the kitchen.

'Rather too much,' Phoebe returned. 'Her mother's dead, her father's never there and someone called Cindy fills in when she feels like it.'

'Cindy,' mused Lynn. 'Someone called Cindy was at Night Birds the other Saturday. People were saying they hadn't seen her around before.'

'What was she like?'

Lynn shrugged. 'Australian, tall, blonde, endless legs,

a bit loud and altogether too keen on other girls' blokes. Not that I noticed her much, you understand.'

Phoebe grinned. 'Naturally. But she doesn't sound the ideal person to be looking after Tara,' she added thoughtfully.

Lynn put her hands on her hips. 'For heaven's sake, Phoebe, lighten up. Haven't you got enough problems of your own?'

'More than enough,' Phoebe agreed ruefully. 'But that doesn't make me indifferent to what's going on in other people's lives.'

'Then maybe it should for once.' Lynn shook her head. 'Listen, the kid is well fed, and extremely well dressed. All her clothes come from Smarty Pants, the boutique in Market Street where my sister works. She has a fiver a day to spend, which is about one hundred per cent more than I ever did at the same age. I'd say she's doing all right.'

'And that's all there is to it?' Phoebe's tone was wry.

'Whether it is or not, there's no reason for you to be involved,' Lynn said sternly. 'Start thinking about yourself instead. Any moment now Debbie will be coming back to work, and you'll be out of a job.'

Phoebe sighed. 'I don't need reminding about that. But I knew when I took it on that it would only be temporary, while Debbie got over her appendicitis.'

Lynn snorted. 'Lazy little cow. If Mrs Preston knew what she was really like, she wouldn't have her back, niece or not.' She paused. 'How's the landlord from hell? Still giving you hassle?'

Phoebe grimaced. 'As ever. He still hasn't done anything about the tile that blew down last month, and now there's a big damp patch on the bedroom ceiling.'

'Does he still snoop around when you're out?'

'I'm sure he does, but I can't prove it,' Phoebe said with exasperation. 'And if I caught him he'd quote his rotten lease at me, saying he has "right of inspection" at any time.'

Lynn shook her head. 'Surely you can find somewhere else?'

'Not until I find a real job as well to go with it. And the problem is there just aren't as many library posts any more, because of all the cutbacks.' Phoebe sighed again. 'I apply for everything, and so far I've made three shortlists and one unsuccessful interview. Maybe I should train for something else.'

'You could always be a teacher,' Lynn suggested. 'You must be good with children. People are always asking you to babysit.'

'That doesn't necessarily mean a thing,' Phoebe said drily. 'All the same, it's an idea. It's just—not what I had planned when I went to university.'

Lynn rolled her eyes expressively round the kitchen. 'And this is?' she mocked. 'By the way, I think your customer's ready to leave.'

It wasn't simply curiosity that made Phoebe follow the child out into the gathering gloom of the November afternoon. It was wrong for Tara to be out on her own at that age, and especially at that time of year. It was growing misty, and the dank chill caught in Phoebe's throat as she watched the small figure scamper up the street.

With a sudden roar, a motorcycle erupted round the corner into High Street and braked violently. Phoebe, shocked and with all her worst forebodings apparently justified, was about to run forward when she saw a tall figure uncoil herself slowly from the pillion seat, giving the child a casual wave. As she took off the helmet she was wearing and handed it back to the driver blonde hair gleamed under the street light.

Cindy, I suppose, thought Phoebe with relief but no particular pleasure. So this is what she does while her charge is roaming free.

The other girl stood talking to the motorcyclist for a moment or two, then blew him a kiss and turned away. Almost at once she and Tara had rounded the corner and disappeared from view.

Oh, well, Phoebe told herself. That's all right, then. And wished she could feel more convinced.

The little house felt cold and damp when she let herself in a couple of hours later. As she switched on the light in the sitting room it flickered, nearly went out, then recovered.

Good, thought Phoebe. Because I don't think I've got a spare bulb.

Unless of course it was the wiring, which would mean another unpleasant interview with her landlord.

I'll worry about that tomorrow, Phoebe decided tiredly.

It wasn't a very comfortable room. It needed decorating, and the square of cheap carpet didn't match the hard two-seater settee with its spindly wooden legs. But she'd laid a fire in the narrow Victorian grate before she'd left for work that morning, and, once it was lit and the curtains drawn, there was a semblance of cosiness.

Not for the first time, Phoebe imagined having some of the things from home there. The rosewood corner cabinet, she remembered sadly, and the Pembroke table and the big winged chair from her father's study. But, like the house itself, they'd gone, sold to pay unexpected and crushing debts.

'I can't believe you could be such a fool, Howard.' She could hear her aunt Lorna's bitter voice now. 'The stock market indeed. Whatever possessed you?'

And her father, sounding quiet and sad. 'I expect I was greedy, like a great many other people, my dear. None of us ever thought it would go wrong.'

'Well, I hope you don't expect Geoffrey and I to help you out of this mess. The recession has hit us too, you know. The most we can do is find you somewhere else to live while you get back on your feet. It will have to be modest, of course, but Geoffrey is prepared to pay a year's rent in advance, and at least it will be a roof over your head. I'm sure one of his business contacts will be able to suggest something suitable.'

'Modest', Phoebe reflected drily, was not the word. Hawthorn Cottage, property of Mr Arthur Hanson, was positively retiring—and singularly lacking in hawthorns or, indeed, any kind of flower or shrub in its miserable strip of concreted-over garden.

'Dad, we can't live here,' she'd whispered as Mr Hanson had grudgingly left them alone 'to get the feel of the place', as he'd put it. 'It's awful.'

'To quote your aunt Lorna, "It's a roof", and it will do while we look round for something better.' He'd hugged her.

Phoebe had been half-heartedly celebrating the end of her finals when her tutor had sent for her. He'd been very kind, very sympathetic, but there had been no way to soften the blow.

Her father had been taken suddenly ill while waiting his turn at the local DSS office. An ambulance had been called, everyone had done what they could, but he'd been dead on his arrival at hospital.

Phoebe, grieving and bewildered, had learned she could stay at the house until the lease was up—but only, she suspected, because Uncle Geoffrey had been unable to retrieve the rent from Hanson the Hateful, as her father had christened him.

She hadn't wanted to stay there—or in Westcombe at all, for that matter—because that part of the country held few happy memories for her. But she'd realised she needed a breathing space. What she had not taken into account was the difficulty of finding work.

She knew how to operate a computer, so she'd managed to keep herself solvent with temping jobs in various offices. But, on the whole, she'd found working at the tea rooms the most congenial.

Mrs Preston might have a blind spot where her niece was concerned, but otherwise her standards were high. Trade was generally brisk, Lynn was down to earth and amusing company and most of the customers had soon seemed like old friends.

She would miss it all very much, but it had never been a prospect for life.

But what was? she asked herself now as she made toast and poached an egg for her supper. Her life had been turned upside down during the past year, and now all she was really sure of was her own uncertainty.

Did she want to be a librarian as she'd always intended? Or should she return to college and take a teaching degree?

I don't know what I want, she thought. And, in those circumstances, Dad always said it was best to do nothing and see what life threw at you.

There was no television in the cottage—Hanson the Hateful claimed the weight of an aerial would damage the chimney—so she listened to the radio as she usually did, then went to bed.

And, for the first time in over a year, she found herself having the dream.

As always there was music playing, somewhere in the distance, and she was floating, weightless, on a bed of clouds, spinning slowly and gently in a gigantic circle, singing softly to herself. There were faces looking down at her, all smiling, and she smiled back, comforted by love and approval, until she saw that all the faces were masked and the smiles painted on, and she tried to run away, and they held her down, their laughter echoing thinly from behind the masks, drowning the music.

And then they all vanished, and he was there—the Dark Lord—staring at her with eyes so cold that they burned.

Shouting at her with words that made no sense, but she knew were full of hatred and contempt.

Threatening her, frightening her with his anger. His disgust.

And she suddenly realised that she was naked and tried to cover herself with her hands, but they were clamped to her sides, and she was spinning again, faster and faster, sinking backwards into some void, trying to hide from the ice and fire of the Dark Lord's eyes. But knowing that there was no escape.

She awoke, sobbing helplessly as she always did, her whole body bathed in sweat.

When she'd regained control, she lay quietly, staring into the darkness, wondering what had prompted a recurrence of her nightmare.

Fitton Magna, she thought, wincing. Tara had said she lived there. That must have been the reason.

But why did it still have to happen? It was six years ago, after all, that devastating, humiliating night. Wasn't it time she laid the memory of it to rest? Surely she wasn't going to be haunted like this for the rest of her life?

The sooner I get away from this whole area and make a completely fresh start, she told herself, the better it will be.

The following day was Friday and market day, and the tea rooms were extra busy.

As the afternoon wore on Phoebe cleared the corner table by the window and put a RESERVED notice on it.

And won't I look a fool if she doesn't turn up? she thought.

But, sure enough, Tara made her appearance at the usual time, and seemed sedately pleased that Phoebe had kept a space for her.

'What's it to be today?' Phoebe smiled down at her.

'Hot milk again? And Mrs Preston's made some chocolate muffins.'

Tara's eyes sparkled. 'Yes, please.'

For a child who seemed to be bringing herself up, she had lovely manners, Phoebe thought as she went to get the order.

After that there was another rush of customers, and it was an hour later that she finally had time to realise that Tara was still sitting at the corner table, staring forlornly through the window.

She checked beside her. 'I'm sorry, poppet. Did you want to pay?'

The child shook her head, looking down and biting her lip. 'I can't. Cindy didn't give me any money today. She said I had to wait here instead until she came. Only she hasn't,' she added on a little wail.

'Don't get upset.' Phoebe passed her a clean paper napkin. 'I'll tell you what. I'll pay the bill for you, and Cindy can settle with me. How's that?'

Tara shook her head. 'We can't do that. I don't know where she is.'

'Well, she can't be too far away. She knows you're waiting.' Phoebe tried to sound casual. 'Is she out with her boyfriend again?'

Tara's eyes looked very big in her small face. 'You aren't meant to know about him. No one is. She'll be cross if she thinks I've told.'

'Well, you haven't,' Phoebe said cheerfully. 'So that's all right. Now, you stay right there, and I'll bring you another muffin. And by the time you've eaten it Cindy will be here for you.'

'What's going on?' Lynn mouthed as she dashed past with a loaded tray.

'Cindy—no show,' Phoebe returned succinctly, and Lynn's brows shot up to her hairline.

But, in spite of her optimistic forecast, no one tall,

blonde and Australian arrived at the tea rooms, and it was rapidly approaching closing time.

'Call the police,' said Lynn. 'That's what Mrs Preston would say.'

'I can't,' Phoebe protested. 'She's upset enough as it is, poor little devil. It could create all kinds of repercussions.'

Lynn sighed. 'Then what are you going to do?'

Phoebe took a deep breath. 'I'll take her home myself. And hopefully give Cindy, and this absentee father of hers, a piece of my mind in the process.'

'You can't just walk off with someone's child. Otherwise it will be you the police will be calling on.'

'That's a risk I'll have to take.' Phoebe looked at the clock above the kitchen door. 'And why isn't there a search party out for her anyway? No, I've got to do it, Lynn. I've got to see her home safely and talk to someone in authority about what's been going on.'

Lynn shook her head. 'Rather you than me.'

As Phoebe had expected, Tara was reluctant to accompany her.

'No, I've got to wait for Cindy.' Her bottom lip jutted ominously.

'But the café is closing for the night,' Phoebe told her gently. 'If Cindy comes it will be all dark and locked up.'

'Then I'll sit in her car and wait.'

Over my dead body, Phoebe returned silently. Aloud, she said, 'Let's go and see if it's still where she parked it, shall we?'

The main car park was emptying fast, and the white Peugeot 205 was standing in the middle, in splendid isolation. It was also securely locked, which Phoebe secretly regarded as a bonus under the circumstances.

However, she was getting more concerned about Cindy's non-appearance by the minute.

'Perhaps her boyfriend's motorbike's had a puncture,'

she suggested neutrally. 'Whatever, there's no point hanging round here in the cold and dark. We'll go round to the bus station and find out when there's one to Fitton Magna.'

But here too she drew a blank. Buses to Fitton Magna, she learned, were thin on the ground. There was one return trip mid-morning and mid-afternoon each day. And a market day special which she'd missed as well.

'Right,' Phoebe said breezily, thanking her stars she'd been paid at lunchtime. 'We'll get a taxi.'

Even if the people at the other end weren't very pleased with what she had to say, they would at least reimburse the fare to her—wouldn't they?

'Do you know the address?' she asked, fixing Tara's seat-belt.

'Of course.' The outraged note was back, if a little wobbly. 'It's North Fitton House.'

'Would that be on the Midburton Road?' the driver asked as he started the engine.

'I don't know,' Phoebe confessed. 'I've never been there.' At least, I hope I haven't, she amended silently. 'Is it, Tara?'

'I think so.' The little girl didn't sound any too sure.

'Well, Fitton Magna isn't exactly big. Reckon we'll find it,' said the driver.

It was a placid drive through the dark lanes, but, all the same, Phoebe could feel tension rising inside her. Beside her, Tara was very quiet. Perhaps too quiet?

I don't really know anything about her, Phoebe realised ruefully. Certainly not enough to go charging in and taking over like this. Lynn was right. I should have stayed out of it. Handed the whole mess over to the police or Social Services.

What do I do if there's no one at her home either? Why didn't I think things through?

There was a muffled sound beside her, as if Tara was choking back a sob, and Phoebe reached out and took a small, cold, shaking hand, squeezing it comfortingly.

'Everything's going to be all right,' she whispered. 'Trust me.'

Knowing, even as she spoke, that in truth she could guarantee nothing.

They were coming to a scatter of houses, lights gleaming behind curtained windows, and Phoebe felt an icy fist clench in her stomach.

Any moment now, she thought, and she might find herself back at the place where the actual scenario of her nightmare had been played out.

But maybe that was what she needed—to go back and exorcise this particular demon once and for all. Let herself see that it was all in the past. That, even if it was the same house where she'd been so bitterly humiliated, the people had changed. Because Tara's name was Vane, and no one called that had been involved.

I would, she told herself, have remembered that.

Ashton, she thought. Dominic Ashton. That had been his name. No Dark Lord of her overheated imagination, but a normal man caught off-guard and reacting furiously to a shameful, tasteless joke.

Who was now somewhere else, living his perfectly normal life, and who had probably never given the incident another thought. Whose biting mouth would twist sardonically in disbelief at the possibility that she could still be tormented by her memories.

It doesn't matter any more, she told herself, drawing a deep breath. I can't afford to let it.

'Well, this is it,' the taxi driver announced.

Leaning forward, Phoebe saw NORTH FITTON HOUSE inscribed on the gate pillar, and, glancing up, the stone gryphon which crowned it. Quite unforgettably.

'Yes,' she said tonelessly. 'This is the place. Could you drive up to the door, please, and wait for me?'

Tara was reluctant to leave the taxi. 'They're going to be so angry.' Her voice caught on a sob.

'But not with you,' Phoebe said bracingly. 'Or they'll have me to deal with.'

She walked forward up the two shallow steps flanked by stone urns, bare now with the onset of winter. On her last visit they'd been a vibrant, sprawling mass of colour which had matched the light and warmth spilling out of the house and her own inner excitement about the party she'd been going to. The man she'd been going to see.

'Sweet Phoebe.' She could hear his voice whispering to her persuasively, overcoming her scruples. 'Promise me you'll be there.'

And I went, Phoebe thought as she rang the bell. Like a lamb to the slaughter.

After a pause, the door was opened by a stout, white-haired woman wearing a dark dress and a neat apron.

'Good evening.' She sounded surprised. 'Can I help...?' Her gaze fell on Tara, clinging to Phoebe's hand, and her hand flew to her mouth.

'Oh, my God, it's the little one. You should have been home hours ago, you naughty girl. I was just going to take your supper up to the nursery. And where's that Cindy, may I ask?'

'You may indeed,' Phoebe said quietly, leading Tara into the hall. 'I've brought Tara home from the café where I work. There seems to have been some mistake over the arrangements to collect her.'

'Mistake,' the other woman repeated. 'And what was Miss Tara doing in a café, I'd like to know? From school to her piano lesson, and then straight home. That's her routine.'

'Apparently not.' Phoebe gave her a level look. 'You mentioned supper, which is a splendid idea. Tara's had rather a trying time, as you can imagine.'

'Well, yes.' The woman looked helplessly from one to the other. 'I don't know what to say, I'm sure.'

'If you could take her upstairs, and see to her.' Phoebe urged the child gently forward. 'Go on, poppet, and I'll come and say goodbye once I've spoken to your father.' She turned to the other woman. 'I presume he's here.'

'Yes, miss, but he's working in his study.' The woman

glanced uneasily at a door on the right of the large hall. 'Left strict instructions he wasn't to be disturbed.'

'I'm sure he did,' Phoebe said with a lightness she was far from feeling. 'But I think this is an emergency, don't you?'

And she walked past them both, opened the study door and went in.

It was a room she remembered only vaguely, with its book-lined walls and the large desk standing in the centre of the room.

He was standing with his back to her, intent on a fax machine delivering a message on a side table.

When he spoke, his voice was clipped with impatience. 'Carrie, I thought I said—'

'It's not Carrie, Mr Vane.' The anger which had been seething in Phoebe came boiling to the surface. 'I've just brought your daughter back from Westcombe, where she'd been abandoned, and I'd like to know whether you're just totally selfish or criminally irresponsible.'

He turned slowly. The grey eyes travelled over her without haste. *Like ice that burned.* She had thought it then. She knew it now.

She gave a gasp, and stepped backwards.

'I don't know who the hell you are, bursting in and abusing me like this.' Every word was like the slash of a whip. 'But you've made a big mistake, young woman.'

He paused, taking in every detail from the top of the smooth brown head, down over her working uniform of white shirt and brief black skirt, to her slender feet in their sensible shoes. Registering it all, then dismissing it with the contempt that she remembered so vividly from six years before.

He said softly, 'My name is Ashton. Dominic Ashton. Now, give me one good reason why I shouldn't throw you out.'

CHAPTER TWO

PHOEBE wanted to run away, harder and faster than she'd ever done in her life. But for dazed seconds she wasn't able to move, or think. She could only stare at him. At the nightmare made flesh, and standing in front of her.

He'd hardly changed at all. She was capable of recognising that, at least. The thick dark hair, untouched by grey, still waved untidily back from its widow's peak. He would never be handsome. His nose was too beaky, his mouth and chin too firmly uncompromising, and the grey eyes under the cynically lifted eyebrows too piercing. But he was even more of a force to be reckoned with than at their last disastrous encounter.

She was the one who'd changed, she realised with a reviving jolt of the same anger which had driven her into this room. She wasn't a naive, betrayed sixteen-year-old any longer.

The real vulnerable child was upstairs, and she was all that mattered in this situation.

She lifted her chin and prayed her voice wouldn't let her down. She probably couldn't equal his own level of contempt in the look she sent him, but, by God, she was going to try.

'The reason—Mr Ashton—is called Tara, and for the past week she's been spending a regular part of the day totally unsupervised in Westcombe.'

The dark brows snapped together. 'What kind of dangerous nonsense is this?'

Phoebe shook her head steadily. 'No nonsense at all. I only wish it were. The girl who looks after her has been allowing her to have tea on her own in the café where I work while she meets her boyfriend.' She paused. 'He has a motorcycle,' she added without expression.

There was a heavy silence. Dominic Ashton was still staring at her, but Phoebe had the feeling that he wasn't seeing her at all.

He said, half to himself, 'I'm going to get to the bottom of this,' and strode towards the door.

Phoebe put up a detaining hand. 'If you're going to look for Cindy, she's not here. At least I don't think she is. She didn't turn up to collect Tara as arranged. And her car is still in the market car park.'

He stopped. Looked down at her. Aware and refocusing, his face suddenly haggard.

She had hated him for six years, for his lack of understanding—and compassion. She had never in the whole of her life expected to feel sorry for him, yet, somehow, she did.

Here he was, in the middle of some business empire, with computers, modems and machinery as far as the eye could see, and just briefly he'd lost his power. He too was naked and bewildered, in a situation he couldn't control.

His voice was quiet. 'I accept what you say—everything you say. But I still think I should check—don't you?' He hesitated. 'Please sit down, Miss—?'

'Grant,' she said. 'Phoebe Grant.'

He nodded, as if storing it for future reference. 'I'll have my housekeeper bring you some coffee.'

'I think she's got her hands full giving Tara her supper.'

'Yes, of course,' he said abruptly. 'I wasn't thinking.' He looked at her again, frowning as if puzzled. 'Where exactly did you say you'd met my daughter?'

'In the Clover Tea Rooms. I'm a waitress there. She sits at one of my tables.' She hesitated. 'I followed her out one afternoon and saw Cindy meet her. That's how I know about the boyfriend. Not through Tara.'

He looked at her as if she were mad. 'What possible difference can that make?'

'Tara promised not to say anything. She's frightened of breaching a confidence.'

'My God,' he said. He pointed at a cupboard. 'You'll find a decanter and glasses. Help yourself to some brandy, and pour one for me. You look as if you need it, and I know I do.'

She said huskily, 'I'm afraid I don't drink.'

'Then perhaps you should start.' The grey eyes examined her critically. 'Or are you always this pale?'

Phoebe looked down at her feet. 'I have a taxi waiting. I'd really like to leave.'

'And I'd be obliged if you'd stay. After all, you marched in, issuing some pretty dire and extremely personal accusations. I'd like the chance to defend myself. But first I need to talk to Tara.' He paused. 'Well?'

Still avoiding his gaze, Phoebe nodded jerkily, and walked to an armchair beside the cheerful fire burning in the grate.

As she heard the door close she felt herself go limp.

'He doesn't remember me,' she whispered to herself. 'He didn't even recognise my name, although in fairness I only gave half of it.'

'Who are you?' he'd demanded with bitter intensity six years before.

And, through a haze of shame and nausea, she'd mumbled, 'Phoebe.'

Of course, she'd looked very different too. Her nondescript brown bob had been concealed under a curly blonde wig then, and her skin had been plastered with make-up.

I thought I looked so glamorous—so sophisticated, she thought sorrowfully. And, instead, I was just being set up.

She shivered, and stretched out her hands to the fire. The burning logs smelled sweet, and the chair was deep and magically comfortable. It would have been very easy to lean back and give herself up to the luxury of the moment. But she couldn't afford to relax.

Dominic Ashton might not have recognised her, but she knew him down to the marrow of her bones. And, when she left here tonight, she wanted him out of her system for good.

If Tara had admitted from the first that her name was really Ashton, would she have the guts to come here and face him tonight? she wondered. Probably not.

But why had Tara told such a pointless fib in the first place? And where had the name 'Vane' come from?

I don't need to know, she reminded herself firmly. I did what I set out to do and made sure Tara was safe. That's as far as it goes. The state of the relationships in this house is none of my business.

But she couldn't help reflecting that clearly the last time she'd seen Dominic Ashton he'd been a married man—Tara would already have been born. Now, it seemed, he was a widower. He'd had more to concern him in the past six years than a trivial prank, however cruel. And the damage caused to herself seemed positively inconsequential compared with what he must have suffered.

Oh, pull yourself together, she thought impatiently. You've allowed yourself the statutory glimmer of compassion. The fact remains that Dominic Ashton was a sadistic, heartless swine six years ago, and the evidence suggests he hasn't undergone any material alteration.

It seemed an eternity before he came back. And, she saw, he was carrying a tray with a silver coffee-pot and two cups which he set down on the desk.

He said, 'I think we should both take a deep breath and start again from scratch.'

Phoebe scrambled awkwardly to her feet, aware that

her skirt had ridden up, revealing more of her long black-clad legs than she wished.

She said rather breathlessly, 'There's really no need for that, Mr Ashton. I did what I thought was necessary, and now I'd just like to leave. My taxi's waiting.'

He shook his head. 'I paid him and sent him away.'

'You did what?' Her voice rose. The realisation that she was as good as trapped here with him made her shake inside. 'You had no right...'

'Oh, please,' he said impatiently. 'Clearly I have every right to establish just what's being going on. And when we've talked I'll run you home myself. It's the least I can do.'

My God, she thought. That's one positively diametric change from our last meeting. You tossed me out then without any regard for what might happen to me. I was little more than a child, and you treated me like a whore.

She said crisply, 'Another cab will be fine. I don't want to drag you away from your important business.' She put ironic emphasis on the last two words.

His brows lifted in swift acknowledgement. 'You really don't think a great deal of me, do you, Miss Grant? Would it earn me some Brownie points if I swore to you that I truly believed when I came home tonight that Tara was safely upstairs in the care of her highly paid nanny?'

'Nevertheless,' Phoebe said stiffly, 'she wasn't your first priority. You didn't actually check.'

'Touché,' he said gravely. 'Now, would you like to drink this coffee, or throw it over me?'

In spite of herself, she felt her lips twitch. He grinned back at her, and she realised it was the first time she'd ever seen him smile.

Realised, too, with a sense of shock, what a powerful attraction he could put out when he tried.

Thank God I'm immune, she told herself as she accepted the cup with a formal word of thanks and reseated herself.

'May I recap on a few points?' Dominic Ashton handed her the cream jug. 'You actually saw Cindy with this guy—how many times?'

'Only once—yesterday. I followed Tara into the street to see where she went. To make sure that she was all right.' Phoebe stirred her coffee.

'It hasn't taken Cindy long to get fixed up,' he said grimly. 'We only moved down here three weeks ago.'

Phoebe moved a restive shoulder. 'I suppose she is allowed a social life.'

'Naturally. She has most weekends off, and usually each evening too. The whole point of moving my business down here was so that I could spend more time with Tara.'

'But I thought—' Phoebe stopped abruptly.

'What did you think?'

She drank some coffee. 'That you'd have to be away a lot on business.'

'Well, it does happen, of course. I was away overnight earlier in the week. But Tara understands, I think. At least I hope she does.'

I wouldn't count on that, Phoebe thought. Aloud, she said slowly, 'She seems very mature for her age. Very self-possessed.'

'In some ways, perhaps.' He looked down at his cup. 'She's had to grow up quickly.'

'Yes.' She hesitated. 'It must have been hard on her— losing her mother like that.'

'You make it sound as if she's been deliberately careless,' he said lightly.

Her lips parted in a silent gasp of outrage. She said thickly, 'I hope you don't refer to your late wife quite so casually in front of Tara.'

'I try not to refer to her at all,' he said curtly, his grey eyes scanning her stormy face. 'And when you talk of my "late" wife, are you referring to Serena's chronic unpunctuality, or are you under the misapprehension that she's departed this life?'

Phoebe nearly spilled her coffee. 'You mean she isn't dead?'

'Good God, no,' he said derisively. 'Only the good die young, Miss Grant. On that assumption, Serena should outlive all of us.'

'Oh, Lord.' Phoebe was scarlet with mortification. 'It's just that Tara said she didn't have a mother, and I assumed...'

Dominic Ashton shrugged. 'It doesn't matter, and in many ways Tara's right. Serena and I have been divorced for the past two years, and she's pursuing her career in California. It was agreed that Tara should remain with me.'

Phoebe said numbly, 'Serena Vane—of course—the actress. I should have realised.'

'I thought you did know. After all, you addressed me as Mr Vane when you came bursting in here.'

Phoebe looked at the floor. 'I—I'm sorry. That must be very—disagreeable.'

'Extremely,' he agreed calmly. 'But during the period of our marriage I became used to it, if not resigned.'

'I saw her in *Tess of the D'Urbervilles* on television,' Phoebe blurted. 'She was wonderful.'

'Yes,' he said. 'Acting is what Serena does best. And I don't blame her for wanting to try her luck in Hollywood.' He paused. 'But I didn't want that life for Tara. Any more than I wanted her to be called that absurd name,' he added, his mouth twisting. 'But Serena was convinced, just before the christening, that she was going to be cast as Scarlett O'Hara in some remake of *Gone with the Wind* that never actually transpired.'

He swallowed the rest of his coffee and put down the cup. 'But I suggest we make a joint vow to make no more assumptions. We're clearly not very good at them. You were convinced that I was an uncaring absentee father, and I assumed that because Cindy was pleasant and came with glowing references that she'd be reliable too.'

'What are you going to do about her?'

He shrugged. 'I'll have to find her first. All her clothes and personal things are still in her room, so I guess she'll be back, sooner or later.'

'And she left the car in the car park.' Phoebe paused for a moment, then said diffidently, 'Perhaps you should phone the local hospitals—and the police. I mean—she could have had an accident.'

'At this precise moment, I'd be glad to hear she'd broken her damned neck. But you're right. I'll start ringing round after I've taken you back.'

She said with a touch of desperation, 'It would save a lot of time and trouble if you'd just get me a taxi.'

'You brought my daughter safely home. I want to do the same for you.'

Which, of course, was unanswerable, Phoebe thought, gritting her teeth.

She said, 'I'd like to say good night to Tara, first, if that's all right.'

'Of course. Whenever you're ready.'

Halfway up the stairs, she began to tremble. What room was Tara going to be in? If it was—that room, then she couldn't go through with it. But then it wouldn't be. Then, as now, it would be the master bedroom.

It was still a relief when they went past the door, Phoebe staring blindly ahead of her. At the far end of the landing, there was another flight of stairs curving away to the left.

'This has always been the nursery suite,' Dominic Ashton said as he led the way. 'Cindy's bedroom is up here too, and a big playroom, and there are two bathrooms, and a kitchenette to make hot drinks and snacks. It's quite self-contained.'

Phoebe murmured something indistinguishable.

Tara was in bed, looking mutinous.

'Carrie said I had to have an early night. But I wanted to come downstairs and play Snakes and Ladders with you and Phoebe.'

Dominic ruffled her hair. 'I'm on Carrie's side. You've had enough fun and games for one day, madam.'

Tara turned pleading eyes on Phoebe. 'Will you come another time and play with me—please?'

This, thought Phoebe, was not part of the plan.

She gave Tara a constrained smile. 'I can't promise anything. I—I do have to work for my living. And you have Cindy to play with.'

'Not any more.' Tara grinned naughtily. 'I heard Daddy tell Carrie that Cindy would come back over his dead body.' Her eyes brightened. 'Daddy, why can't Phoebe be my nanny instead?'

There was a silence. Then Dominic said easily, 'I'm sure she has a hundred reasons. I'll leave her to tell you some of them while I make a few phone calls.'

'Don't you really and truly want to be my nanny?' Tara asked when they were alone. 'I thought you liked me.'

'I do like you.' Phoebe sat on the edge of the bed. 'But it isn't that simple. I have a job already.'

'But it's much nicer here than it is in that café,' Tara urged. 'You'd have a lovely bedroom. Would you like to look at it?' She began to scramble out of bed, and Phoebe restrained her firmly.

'And I have a home, too.' *With a roof that leaks and wiring on the blink and a nosy landlord.* 'Your father will soon find someone else to look after you.'

'I don't want someone else.' Tara sounded rebellious and fractionally close to tears.

Phoebe took her hand. 'Look, I came to say good night, not have a fight. Everything will work out, poppet. You'll see.'

Tara pulled her hand away and turned over, burying

her face in the pillow. 'I don't like being on my own,' said a muffled voice.

Phoebe sighed soundlessly. 'Listen, if you're a good girl, and stop fussing, I'll come and play Snakes and Ladders with you one day. If your daddy will let me, that is.'

A transformed and beaming face was lifted from the pillow. 'Will you come tomorrow?'

'No, I have to go to work. Besides,' she added with a touch of sternness, 'Saturdays and Sundays are your special time with your father, aren't they?'

'Ye-e-es.' Tara wriggled a bit. 'But he wouldn't mind if you were there too.'

'Oh, I think he might,' Phoebe said lightly. *And I certainly should.* 'Cuddle down now, and I'll tuck you in.'

Tara obeyed. 'You sound like a nanny,' she said.

Phoebe bent and swiftly kissed a pink cheek. 'That's the easy part,' she said.

She closed the door softly behind her, and started down to the floor below. All the doors were shut there too, but she could remember what the rooms were like, she thought, her footsteps faltering a little. Especially one of them. The one with the big four-poster bed with a canopy over it. The one she'd been taken to...

Out of the past, she could remember someone saying, 'It looks like a bloody altar.'

And Tony's voice drawling, 'Then let's supply the virgin sacrifice.'

She shivered violently, trying to blot out his voice as well as the more potent memories of his lips on hers, his hands moving over her, undressing her slowly...

'Is something the matter?' Dominic Ashton's voice, speaking sharply, broke across her reverie.

She realised she was standing, rooted to the spot, outside his bedroom. He was at the top of the stairs, staring at her.

He said, 'I've never heard that this house is haunted, but you look as if you've seen a ghost.'

'No—no, I'm fine. I—I thought I heard Tara calling,' she improvised rapidly.

He said abruptly, 'I'll sleep up there tonight, in case she needs anything.'

Phoebe walked ahead of him down to the hall. 'You don't think there's a chance Cindy will turn up?'

'I know she won't,' he said grimly. 'You were quite right. She's in hospital—and the boyfriend too. I've just been on to the casualty department at Westcombe. They had an accident on the bike—hurrying back for Tara, apparently.'

Phoebe gasped. 'Are they badly hurt?'

'Torn ligaments for him, and a broken collarbone for her. It could have been very much worse. I'll call in there after I've dropped you off, with a dose of unpleasant medicine for the pair of them.'

She said quickly, 'Don't be too angry with her, please. She'll know how stupid she's been, and be feeling really bad about it. And anger's such an awful thing—when you're frightened and ashamed, anyway...' Her voice tailed into silence.

'Well,' he said at last. 'That was certainly a cry from the heart.' He held out her coat for her. 'Do I really seem so formidable?'

'I—I was speaking generally.' Phoebe slid her arms into the sleeves and began to fumble with the buttons.

'Were you?' His grey gaze was searching. 'I'd have said you had something very particular in mind, and—'

To her intense relief, his analysis was interrupted by a sharp peal of the doorbell.

Dominic Ashton's brows rose. 'Now, who can this be?' he said, half to himself.

He went to the door and threw it open.

'Darling.' The woman who swept in with immense assurance was tall, with pale blonde hair swept back by a velvet Alice band. Her wine-coloured cape swirled around her. 'Mummy and Daddy are having an impromptu drinks party—such fun—and—' she gave a girlish laugh '—they've sent me over to scoop you up.'

Now that, thought Phoebe, her own troubles forgotten in sudden relish, is something I'd really like to see. Dominic Ashton didn't seem a man who'd 'scoop' easily.

He said courteously, 'Good evening, Hazel. That's very kind of you all, but I'm afraid I'm not available tonight. We've had a slight domestic crisis.'

'Oh, dear.' The newcomer's rather prominent blue eyes focused on Phoebe, taking in her ordinary appearance and the elderly waxed jacket she was wearing. 'Have I arrived at an awkward moment? Are you in the process of firing a member of your staff? I can wait in the car till you've finished.'

'No,' Dominic said pleasantly. 'Actually that's not it. This is Phoebe Grant, who doesn't work for me in any capacity. Miss Grant, may I introduce you to Hazel Sinclair, who's the daughter of some neighbours of mine?'

Phoebe murmured, 'How do you do?' and, in return, was given a bright smile which revealed very white teeth.

'All the better to eat you with, Grandma,' she said under her breath.

The social niceties concluded, Hazel Sinclair returned to her prey. 'So what's the problem, my pet? Is there anything I can do to help?'

He shook his head. 'I doubt it. Tara's nanny's made rather a fool of herself and ended up in hospital.'

'Oh, these ghastly girls.' She flung her hands in the air. 'I really don't know how anyone copes with them. And I have to say she always did seem rather—flighty to me. Now, what you want is an older woman, a nanny of the old school, who'd keep a firm hand on poor little Tara.'

'Is that what you think she needs?' Dominic asked mildly.

'All small girls do, my dear.' She tapped him roguishly on the arm. 'Especially charmers like your Tara, who can twist their fathers round their little fingers. She's a delight, but you must be careful not to—overcompensate for the fact you're a one-parent family.'

'I am aware of that,' he said, a touch drily. 'I thought until an hour or so ago that I'd got the balance about right. Until Miss Grant arrived to correct me, that is.'

'Oh, really?' Phoebe found herself subjected to a somewhat sharper scrutiny. 'Are you some kind of social worker, then?'

'No,' Phoebe said. 'I'm a waitress at the Clover Tea Rooms, in Westcombe.'

'I see.' Hazel Sinclair clearly didn't. She gave a silvery laugh. 'It's not an establishment I'm familiar with, I have to say. Is it one of your haunts, Dominic? It doesn't sound very likely.'

'It isn't,' he said briefly. 'But Tara likes it, apparently.' He paused. 'I don't want to seem ungracious, Hazel, but I was just about to run Miss Grant back to Westcombe and then visit the hospital.'

'Of course. I must be getting back myself. The first guests will be arriving.' She smiled at him dazzlingly. 'If you've time when you've completed all your errands of mercy, call round. So many people want to welcome you back after all this time. Besides, it's essential for you not to be a hermit.'

'I think I can promise that.' He took the hand she'd archly extended and dropped a quick kiss on it. 'Tonight just isn't on, Hazel, but I'll ring you next week and we'll have dinner.'

'I'll hold you to that, darling.' She bestowed a distinctly less radiant look on Phoebe. 'Goodnight, Miss—er...?'

'Grant,' Phoebe supplied helpfully. 'Clover Tea Rooms. Home-baking a speciality.'

As he closed the front door behind Hazel Dominic Ashton turned back to Phoebe with a wintry look.

'You're not quite as demure as you look, are you, Miss Grant?'

'I don't understand.' Phoebe returned the look. 'Is there a problem?'

There was a brief, oddly pregnant silence, then he said slowly, still staring at her, 'Do you know, Miss Grant? I think there might be. I really think there might.'

He sighed, swiftly and sharply. 'So—shall we go now?'

'Please,' said Phoebe. And thought, The sooner, the better.

CHAPTER THREE

IT WAS a largely silent journey. Dominic Ashton seemed lost in thought as he expertly threaded his powerful four-wheel drive through the lanes.

And Phoebe, sitting with her hands clenched tightly in her lap, was far too uncomfortably aware of his physical proximity to be capable of producing any intelligent topic of conversation to fill the void.

'Only six weeks until Christmas,' and, 'Do you think we'll have snow before New Year?' were all she could think of, and she instantly discarded both of them. Silence was preferable to total banality.

'Whereabouts in Westcombe?' he eventually asked abruptly as they approached the outskirts.

'You can drop me in the High Street.'

'I could also throw you in the river,' he observed icily. 'But, as I intend to take you to your door, let's drop the evasions and give me your address. It will save us both time and temper.'

'Hawthorn cottage—twenty-nine, Rushton Street,' Phoebe said eventually, and mutinously.

'Simplest solutions are always best,' he murmured, and her hands curled into fists.

Hang in there, she adjured herself silently. A few more minutes and he'll be gone. And as soon as Debbie comes back to work you can go too—as far and as fast as possible. And you'll never, ever have to see him again.

As they drew up, she said, 'Thank you.'

'I wish I could think you meant that.' He leaned forward, studying the narrow little house crammed awkwardly between its neighbours. 'Astonishing.'

'I beg your pardon?' Phoebe felt herself bristling.

'Granted.' He swung himself lithely out of the driving seat and went round to open the passenger door. 'I was thinking what a strange mass of contradictions you are.'

'Well, please don't lose any sleep over it, Mr Ashton,' she snapped, ignoring the helping hand he'd extended as she scrambled out.

'On the contrary,' he said softly. 'I have a strong feeling that you're going to cost me a lot of sleepless nights, Miss Grant.'

Phoebe, shaken, and for once at a loss, gave him a fulminating look and stalked to her gate.

As she opened it she heard, quiet but unmistakable, the creak of her front door closing. She stopped dead with a groan. 'Oh, no.'

'I'll deal with it.' Dominic Ashton strode past her towards the shadowy figure hovering in the porch.

Phoebe, close on his heels, heard a slight scuffle and a yelp. 'Oh, don't hurt him. It's my landlord.'

'But he was coming out of your house.'

'She's been complaining about a leak in the roof,' Arthur Hanson squeaked in breathless outrage. He was a thin man, balding, with a straggling beard. 'I came round to look at it.'

'In the pitch darkness?' Dominic asked contemptuously. 'You haven't even got a flashlight.'

'I decided to have a look in the loft first,' Mr Hanson said, with an attempt at dignity.

'In Miss Grant's absence?' Dominic released his hold on the other man's collar.

'He's always doing it,' Phoebe said wearily.

'I have a right to conduct regular inspections.'

'From now on, telephone Miss Grant and make an appointment.'

As Mr Hanson scuttled off Dominic turned a frowning gaze on Phoebe. 'Has this been going on for long?'

'Ever since I moved in.'

'Then I strongly recommend you have the locks changed. He may be your landlord, but you have a right to your privacy.'

He followed her into the hall, looking around him critically. Comparing it, no doubt, with North Fitton House. 'How much rent is he charging you?'

Phoebe lifted her chin. 'Isn't that covered by the right to privacy you just mentioned?' she challenged.

'It's not just idle curiosity. I have contacts in the private rental market,' he said. 'I'm sure you could get something better than this.'

'It's perfectly adequate for my present needs,' she said stiffly.

'And your job represents complete fulfilment too?' There was a note of faint derision in his voice.

She shrugged defensively. 'I like my colleagues, and the customers are pleasant.'

'Give or take the odd waif and stray.'

'Tara was hardly that.' She paused. 'Please don't let me keep you, Mr Ashton. You must be keen to get to the hospital. I don't know when visiting hours end...'

'There's plenty of time.' His mouth curved in amusement. 'You're not very subtle, Miss Grant. Or very hospitable,' he added. 'Considering I've driven you home, and got rid of a pest for you.'

'I didn't ask you to do either.' Phoebe jiggled the sitting-room light switch in increasing irritation. 'I don't need your help, Mr Ashton. I can handle my own affairs.'

'In the same way as you're dealing with that light, I suppose?' With infuriating coolness, he moved her gently out of the way, clicked the switch and the light stuttered on. He looked, frowning, at the old-fashioned flex supporting the central pendant. 'Does that happen much?'

'It's temperamental,' she conceded.

'Perhaps it's the effect you have on it,' he murmured. 'Does the kettle not work either?'

There was a silence, then Phoebe took a deep breath. 'May I offer you some coffee, Mr Ashton?' she asked grimly.

'How kind of you, Miss Grant,' he mocked. 'I thought you'd never ask.'

So did I, Phoebe thought, seething as she went down the narrow passage to the kitchen.

She was totally aware of him, lounging in the doorway, watching her, as she filled the kettle and set it to boil. She had fresh coffee and a percolator, but instant would do for this occasion, she thought, getting down the jar and spooning granules into two mugs. Instant coffee and, hopefully, instant departure. Certainly she'd give him no excuse to linger.

But as she added the milk he'd politely requested, and stirred the brew, she had the uneasy feeling that he knew exactly what she was up to, and was laughing at her.

Jaw set, she led the way back to the sitting room, pausing in surprise to see that he'd kindled the fire.

'I believe there's a superstition that you shouldn't tend anyone's fire until you've known them for seven years, but I decided to risk it,' Dominic Ashton drawled. 'After all, we're practically old acquaintances.'

Her heart skipped a panicky beat. 'Not,' she said, 'as far as I'm concerned.'

His mouth twisted. 'You don't take many prisoners, Phoebe.' He paused. 'That's an unusual and charming name. May I know how you came by it? Or is that another invasion of privacy?'

Phoebe looked at the flickering fire. 'My mother was playing the shepherdess in an amateur production of *As*

You Like It when she met my father,' she said, her voice unconsciously wistful. 'It was love at first sight.'

'Even though Phoebe isn't a very likeable character in the play?'

She was startled. 'You know Shakespeare?'

'I'm not a complete Philistine.' Leaning back on the cramped settee, his long legs stretched out in front of him, he dwarfed the room. 'Where are your parents now?'

Phoebe sank her teeth into her lower lip. Then she told him, 'My mother died when I was a child. I—I lost my father just over six months ago.'

He closed his eyes for a moment. 'Oh, God, I'm sorry. My facetious remarks about Serena were totally out of place.'

'You couldn't have known,' she said. 'Please don't worry about it.'

'Have you any brothers or sisters?'

She shook her head. 'I was an only child.'

'No relations at all?' He was frowning.

'My father's sister is still alive,' she said. 'But we're not close.' She paused. 'My father put all his energies into work after my mother—went. He was very successful, and eventually sold his business for a great deal of money. He should have been secure for life. He invested in a second-hand bookshop, which he ran himself as a hobby. He was really happy, probably for the first time in years.'

'And?' he prompted when she hesitated.

'Only someone persuaded him to play the stockmarket. He ended up owing enormous sums—debts he couldn't possibly pay. We lost everything. The house, the shop, the furniture—it was all sold off.'

She shook her head. 'My aunt seemed to feel that Dad had shamed the family name, and she wrote us off, even though he'd helped her husband out several times in the past.'

'And she wasn't prepared to do the same, and couldn't live with the guilt,' he said calmly. 'It's quite a familiar story.'

A story that she couldn't believe she'd actually told him. It was something, like her grief, which she'd kept private, hugged fiercely to herself. She'd never confided in anyone. How had he, of all people, managed to break through the shell?

She gathered her defences. 'What do you know about it?'

'I come across similar cases all the time in my work. I'm a financial adviser—a troubleshooter, if you like. I go into companies, large and small, which have hit problems, and try and provide realistic solutions.'

'I hope,' she said, 'that you don't look at me in the same light.'

'Certainly not,' he said. 'Your path is clearly strewn with primroses.'

'Because,' she went on, as if he hadn't spoken, 'I don't need your charity.'

'And I wouldn't dream of offering it,' he said coolly. 'I'm very highly paid for what I do.'

'Encouraging people at their wits' end to get into more debt?' she said bitterly. 'Raising false hopes?'

He finished his coffee and set down his mug. He said slowly, 'Your poor opinion of me seems to have all kinds of ramifications.'

'We're strangers,' she said. 'I don't have an opinion.'

'Lady, you could have fooled me,' he drawled. 'I'd say I was tried and condemned before you ever set eyes on me.' He leaned forward, his grey eyes fixed on her face.

'Today,' he said. 'You did me a tremendous service. When we were at my house, I suggested that we make a fresh start. I'd still like to do that.'

'Why?' she asked baldly.

'Because I want to be your friend.' He spoke very

gently. His eyes were gentle too, and his mouth curved suddenly in a smile without mockery. Despite herself, Phoebe felt a sudden pang of emotion akin to longing twist deep inside her. And it frightened her.

She said tonelessly, 'That's very obliging of you, Mr Ashton. But I have enough friends already.'

'Indeed.' He got to his feet. 'Well,' he went on, his face and voice expressionless, 'that must make you unique to the rest of the human race. Then can I ask instead that you don't consider me an enemy when we meet in future?'

Phoebe rose too. 'It's unlikely our paths will ever cross again, Mr Ashton.'

'I'm sorry to hear that because I know Tara has her heart set on seeing you.' He walked to the door, then turned. He said quietly, 'Phoebe, please don't allow your judgement of me to affect my daughter. That wouldn't be fair. Goodnight.'

She heard the front door close behind him, and sank back onto her chair, aware that her legs were shaking under her.

'And that's not fair either,' she whispered under her breath. 'Oh, so clever, Mr Ashton.'

She couldn't sleep that night, although she tried the usual anodynes of a warm bath and hot chocolate. She found herself tossing restlessly from one side of the bed to the other.

Dominic Ashton filled her mind, precluding all else.

She could hardly believe her own bad luck. On his own admission, he'd only been back at Fitton Magna a short time. If she hadn't been offered that temporary job at the tea rooms, she might have moved away from Westcombe in complete safety, her peace of mind intact.

Peace of mind? a scornful voice in her head seemed to ask. You don't even know what that means. For six years you've been torturing yourself over this man.

Doing endless penance for something that wasn't even your fault. Flaying yourself over a humiliation that he doesn't even remember. Not even your name rang any bells with him. It was all far too trivial for that. You've been beating yourself to death for nothing, you stupid bloody idiot.

And now you've seen him again. You've talked to him and the world hasn't come to an end. In fact, this could just be the impetus you need to get you out of Westcombe and onto this new life that you want. If you're not careful, you could end up feeling grateful to him.

'Oh, no,' Phoebe said aloud, and forcefully. 'Not that. Never that.'

She pushed the quilt away, got out of bed, put on her robe and trailed downstairs.

There were still embers glowing in the grate, and she added a few sticks and some lumps of coal, then curled up in the corner of the settee, staring at the flames.

Whatever she did, the bad dreams, the obsession with Dominic Ashton as the villain who had scarred her for life had got to end, she told herself. And that wouldn't happen unless she went back to the beginning. Remembered, and placed in perspective, everything that had happened.

Up to now, she'd never really allowed herself to do that, telling herself it hurt too much. Finding it easier to focus only on the culmination of the whole wretched chain of events.

Now she made herself recall how it had all begun.

Which, of course, had been with Tony...

'You fancy him, don't you?' asked Tiffany, laughing.

Phoebe blushed. 'No, of course not.'

They were in Tiffany's bedroom, trying on clothes. Phoebe looked at herself in a tiny scarlet Lycra skirt and a black bustier. She'd never worn anything like them in her life. She'd never been allowed to. Her father was ultra-conservative about clothes. When Phoebe needed anything, a personal shopper from one of the big department stores was employed and her instructions were clear.

In fact, it was amazing that her dad had allowed her to spend a few days at Tiffany's. But then, as she admitted to herself, if he'd had any idea what a comparatively short time Phoebe had known her, he would probably have refused. The fact that Tiffany had only arrived at the school the previous term had been kept strictly under wraps.

Tiffany's house was a revelation. It had been designed along the lines of an ante-bellum mansion of the American Deep South, because, as Tiffany's mother had explained, she'd spent her honeymoon in New Orleans and felt it was her spiritual home.

The decor was lavish. Phoebe, more used to book-lined walls and faded chintzes, thought, a shade uncomfortably, that it was like a Hollywood movie set. Every bathroom gleamed with gold fittings. Every window seemed to droop under the sheer weight of swagged and festooned velvet. The kitchen seemed as elaborate as the control capsule of a space craft, and as sterile, because no one ever cooked in it.

Outside, there was a heart-shaped swimming pool, with an adjoining Jacuzzi, and a tennis court.

Partly because of this, but mainly through the totally casual welcome extended by the Bishops to anyone who turned up, the place was always teeming with people.

Tony Cathery was one of them.

He was at university, reading Fine Arts, because, as he'd said, he couldn't think of anything more useful, and Tiffany, apparently, had known him 'for ever'.

He was tall and blond, with blue eyes which crinkled at the corners, and a glossy Mediterranean tan acquired in the Greek islands earlier that summer. And, yes, he'd confirmed, grinning, it was all over, if anyone wanted to check. He was a marvellous swimmer, a terrific tennis player and an exuberantly sexy dancer.

Phoebe had never encountered anyone quite like him. Up to the time of his arrival, she'd been feeling very much the odd one out. There was no one else she knew there, and everyone else seemed so much smarter and streetwise than she did.

She was miserably aware that a couple of the girls had christened her 'Feeble Feeb' and laughed at her behind her back, and there had been times when she'd wondered if Tiffany was regretting that she'd ever invited her. Certainly she didn't seem to want to spend much time with her. And, in a house virtually devoid of books, Phoebe often found herself at a loss.

Eventually, she discovered an elaborate onyx and ivory chess set on a table in the ornate conservatory which served as an extension of the drawing room.

She was hunched over it one day, half-heartedly working out a chess problem—and considering the more pressing dilemma of what excuse she could make to cut her visit short—when a voice behind her said softly, 'My God, I don't believe it. At last, a woman with a brain.'

Startled, Phoebe turned to find Tony Cathery smiling down at her.

'Black seems to be in a hopeless position,' he went on, pulling up a chair opposite her. 'Let's see what I can do.'

By the time the problem was solved, Phoebe was shyly hanging on his every word.

That night he sat beside her at dinner, and made her join in the dancing afterwards. Phoebe could see the surprise on the other girls' faces, and revelled in it.

Not so Feeble Feeb, she thought joyously.

But she was also a little nervous. Her sexual experience, apart from a few kisses, was nil. She might be dazzled, but she was also wary, unsure what Tony wanted from her.

But Tony, oddly, seemed wary too—hesitant to push things too far or too fast between them—and she was grateful for his restraint, at first anyway. Then, as time went on, she began to wonder. To worry a little.

She was cheered, however, when he told her there was going to be a party the following Friday evening at a house some miles away.

'You are going to come with me, aren't you?' he asked almost anxiously.

'I haven't been invited. Besides, I said I'd go home at the weekend.'

Tony groaned. 'Oh, sweetheart, you can't do this to me. Ring home. Say you're staying on for a few days.' He put his hand on the nape of her neck, under the heavy fall of brown hair, and stroked the slender curve very gently, making her body arch in delight.

He put his lips to her ear, and whispered, 'I don't want to part with you, darling. Not yet.'

The next day, she phoned her father, making some excuse, trying not to hear the disappointment in his voice.

Because she needed to be with Tony. She couldn't bear to leave either. Not before...

Always, at that point, her mind closed off.

She believed that Tony must want her, otherwise why would he spend so much time exclusively with her? She just wished he would show it rather more openly. Each time he kissed her, he seemed to be holding back. The caresses he offered were exciting, but fleeting too, always short of any real intimacy, leaving her unsatisfied and longing for more.

And she had other, minor worries too. She wanted to look wonderful for Tony at the party, but she was dismally aware that he'd seen all the clothes she'd brought with her, and there was nothing sensational among them.

So, when Tiffany had asked her casually what she was planning to wear, and she'd confessed she didn't know, she'd found herself immediately up in Tiffany's room, confronted with a whole range of the kind of gear that looked so terrific on the others.

'Well, he certainly fancies you.' Tiffany, lounging on the bed, wouldn't let the topic rest.

Phoebe tried pulling her hair up on top of her head, but it was too heavy and too thick, and kept sliding down again.

She sighed. 'I don't think so.'

'That's crap. He never leaves you alone.'

Phoebe sighed again. 'Actually, he does. He treats me as if I was made of glass and might break.'

'He wouldn't if he saw you dressed like that,' Tiffany giggled.

'But he won't see me.' Phoebe tried not to sound desolate.

'Of course he will.' Tiffany sat up. 'Y'know, your problem is that you give off the wrong vibes. The way you dress and talk and present yourself all says "hands off", and guys like Tony pick that up. So, on Friday, you're going to give him a signal that says "I'm available". And I'm going to help.'

Phoebe gave her a quick, rather shamefaced look. 'Are you sure, Tiff? It's just that I thought—at the beginning—that it was Tony and you...'

Tiffany laughed. 'Hardly. We know each other far too well.' She contemplated Phoebe with a satisfied smile, like the cat with the cream. 'Put yourself in my hands, and you'll knock his eyes out on Friday.'

Phoebe could hardly believe her own eyes when she was finally allowed to look in the mirror on Friday evening. Her own hair was concealed under a shoulder-length blonde wig, which Tiffany had purloined from her mother's room. Her eyes were slumbrous with kohl, and her lips gleamed a deep, wicked red.

'You look more like Madonna than she does,' said Tiffany.

Downstairs, Phoebe was disappointed to discover that Tony had gone ahead to the party with some of the others.

'Whose party is it, anyway?' she asked Tiffany, who shrugged vaguely.

'Just the usual bash,' she returned. 'Don't worry about it.'

She'd expected the house to be another designer nightmare, like Tiffany's, so North Fitton House came as a pleasant surprise. She lingered on the steps, breathing in the fragrance of the night-scented stocks which filled the stone urns flanking the front door.

Tiffany gave her a little push. 'Come on. There's a hungry man waiting in there.'

Tony's reaction was all that she could have desired.

'You look fantastic,' he muttered, his eyes resting hotly on the cleavage revealed by the bustier. 'Absolutely perfect.' He licked his lips. 'Tiff—you're a genius.'

She heard Tiffany say with a giggle, 'And now the rest is up to you.'

Tony grabbed Phoebe's hand and pulled her into one of the rooms. 'What do you want to drink?'

'Just orange juice,' she assured him hurriedly.

'Whatever my princess requires,' he said.

In the end, she was sorry she'd asked for it because it tasted odd. She would have poured it into one of the jardinières in the drawing room, given half a chance, but Tony was close beside her all the time. And the next one didn't taste nearly as bad, and the one after that was actually pleasant, so she thought she must have imagined it. Or maybe it was a brand she hadn't come across before.

'Whose party is this?' she asked Tony while they were dancing.

He shrugged. 'Just a guy I know. It's his birthday, so we thought we'd surprise him.'

'Oh.' Phoebe was puzzled. 'Which one is he?'

'He hasn't arrived yet,' Tony said easily. 'He's had to go to some boring dinner first, but he'll be along later and then you'll meet him, I promise.' He drew her closer, running practised fingers down her bare back. 'In the meantime, just concentrate on me.'

Deliriously, Phoebe obeyed. She had never dreamed this could happen. That Tony would be holding her like this, his lips nuzzling her neck, creating all kinds of strange, delicious sensations deep within her.

It was a hot night, and the rooms were crowded, so she was glad of the orange juice, and grateful to Tony for keeping her so assiduously supplied.

In fact, the room was far too hot, because her head was swimming and her legs were behaving strangely. Her voice sounded odd too. Slurred and far away, as if she were speaking in an echo chamber.

'C'n I sit down a minute?'

'Oh, we can do better than that.' Tony's arm was like an iron bar round her waist, supporting her. She realised they were going upstairs.

'Where's thish?'

'I'm taking you to lie down,' he murmured. 'It's cooler up here, and you'll feel better soon.'

He opened a door. The big, canopied bed which dominated the room seemed to sway in front of her.

'The master bedroom,' Tony said exultantly. 'Now, all we need is the master.'

The bed felt as soft as a cloud as she stretched out upon it.

'It looks like a bloody altar.'

'Then let's supply the virgin sacrifice.'

The words made no sense to her. As Tony came to lie beside her she turned to him greedily, offering the softness of her mouth.

'Oh, I'm tempted,' he said thickly. 'Believe me, I am.'

'That's not the deal.' It seemed to be Tiffany's voice. 'You're having me—remember?'

Phoebe opened dazed eyes, and found the room revolving slowly. There were people standing round the bed. She could see their mouths smiling, but she couldn't recognise any of the faces. The room was going faster, and she mumbled, 'Make it shlow down.'

'Anything you say, Princess.' Tony's hands were caressing her just as she'd always dreamed. She could feel him undoing all the little buttons on the bustier. Dimly, she could hear voices and laughter, and a few whistles.

Tony was kissing her bare breasts, sucking hard on her nipples, hurting her, so that she moaned a little and tried to pull away.

'You're wasting time.' Tiffany's voice again.

There were other hands on her now, pulling down her skirt. She resisted, protesting weakly.

Someone said, 'You can have your clothes back now, Tiff.'

And Tiffany's reply, swift and venomous. 'After she's been wearing them? You're joking.'

'Tony,' Phoebe whispered, bewildered. 'Wass happening? Where are you?'

She heard his voice. 'I'm here. Close your eyes, Princess.'

She was glad to obey, and shut out the staring faces. It stopped the room revolving too, which was also a relief.

But her mouth felt so dry. She ran her tongue round her lips. 'I—I need a drink.'

'No more for you, Princess. We don't want you unconscious for your big moment.'

She wondered fuzzily what he meant. Nothing made sense any more. All she wanted was for everyone to go away, and Tony to take her in his arms again. Not hurting her, but gentle, like he'd been in the past.

After a while, the whispering and giggling seemed to fade away, and there was nothing but silence and darkness...

I want to stop there, Phoebe thought, gathering the folds of her robe around her with a shiver. I don't want to remember any more. But I must. I have to deal with it—all of it—once and for all time.

And then I can get on with the rest of my life.

But first—first, I have to think about Dominic.

CHAPTER FOUR

PHOEBE was grateful at first for the quiet and the shadows. She felt light-headed, weightless, rocked on some infinite, swaying ocean. Soon, she thought drowsily, soon Tony would return. She lay back on the pillows, smiling to herself. Waiting for him. Wanting him.

The sudden brilliance of the overhead light snapping on was like a physical shock. She propped herself groggily on one elbow, staring towards the door.

Not Tony at all, she registered dazedly, but a complete stranger in dinner jacket and frilled shirt, his black tie unfastened.

A tall man, with dark hair and eyes as grey and cold as a January sky. A man standing there as if he'd been transfixed. Clearly as startled as she was herself.

His gaze grated across her skin. He said slowly and harshly, 'What the hell are you doing here?'

The room was swaying again. She stared frantically past him, searching for Tony—for anyone except this unknown man who was looking at her as if she was dirt. As if he despised her.

And then, in the long mirror beside the door, she saw herself, irrevocably and indelibly, as he did—naked and bedraggled, her face under the dishevelled blonde wig flushed and streaked with make-up. Someone she barely recognised, but knew must be herself.

He took a step closer and she shrank, grabbing at a sheet to cover herself. 'I said—what are you doing here? And who are you?'

'Phoebe,' she mumbled from her dry throat. 'I'm Phoebe. Tony—brought me.'

He said bitterly, 'I should have known. Well, you're wasting your time. I can do without your kind of filth.' He bent, picked up the handful of her discarded clothing lying beside the bed, his mouth grim with distaste, and threw it at her. 'Get dressed and get out, you slut, before I throw you out.'

He walked across the room and flung open another door. Phoebe could see gleaming tiles and the edge of a bath.

'And dress in there,' he went on bitingly. 'I don't want to watch.'

She couldn't move. She felt numb, paralysed with horror. She had to say something—to explain that it was all a terrible mistake. But the words wouldn't come. She could only stare up at him helplessly.

He completely misinterpreted her lack of response. Phoebe found herself ruthlessly dragged off the bed by her arm and pushed forcefully into the bathroom.

'No more games,' he told her. 'You have exactly ten minutes to make yourself decent, or I call the police.'

The door slammed behind her. Phoebe looked at the grotesque caricature of her own face in the mirror above the wash-basin, and was instantly and comprehensively sick.

She had never been so ill. Each wave of nausea seemed more bitter, more all-engulfing than the last. And even when her stomach was empty she was still clinging to the lavatory bowl, retching weakly.

Eventually, she levered herself to her feet, splashed her face with cold water and put on her underwear. She mentally recoiled when she came to the outer clothing, but there was nothing else to choose, so reluctantly she dragged on the skirt and fastened the bustier. Her shaking fingers could hardly cope with the myriad buttons, but she persevered, urged on by his threat of the police. That, she thought, visualising her father's horrified face, would be the ultimate degradation.

She was ready at last—for whatever might be facing her, she thought, swallowing. Slowly, she opened the bathroom door and looked into the room beyond. It was empty. The bed, she saw, was stripped of everything—even the pillows and duvet. Gone to be decontaminated, no doubt, she thought, supporting herself against the doorframe, fighting another wave of nausea.

She went out onto the landing and cautiously down the stairs. She felt raw and hollow inside, and her throat ached with vomiting.

The house was ominously quiet. No music, no sound of voices. Where was everyone? she thought, fighting down a feeling of panic.

He was waiting in the hall below, the dark face carved from stone.

'Where are the others?' Her voice was hoarse and strained.

'Long gone.'

Gone? she thought numbly. Leaving her behind? But they couldn't...

'Who are you?' she asked.

He tutted. 'Didn't they tell you that? I'm Dominic Ashton, and this—shambles you're about to vacate is my property.' He tossed her bag to her. 'This must be yours.'

Then he walked to the front door and opened it, letting in a wave of cold night air. Despite herself, Phoebe shivered.

'A word of advice,' the hated, contemptuous voice went on. 'Next time you go whoring, try and stay sober. It makes a better impression on the client.'

She said hoarsely, 'I'm not—what you think.'

'You're certainly not very good at it.' He gestured impatiently. 'Now get out.'

'But how am I going to get back?' She knew exactly what her bag contained—a lipstick, a comb, a hanky and a few coins. 'I've no transport. I haven't even got a jacket.'

'That's your problem,' was the curt dismissal. 'Presumably you got paid for your—services tonight. There's a call box in the village with the names of local cab firms.'

'I'm not a whore,' she said desperately. 'I swear I'm not. I—I was with—Tony. No one gave me any money.'

There was a taut silence, then he reached inside his jacket, produced a wallet and extracted a twenty-pound note, which he dropped onto the carpet in front of her.

'For the floorshow,' he said insolently, the grey eyes raking her, reminding her starkly of how he'd found her—stripped and vulnerable on his bed.

She wanted to hit him, to lash out with her nails and wipe the mockery from his face. But she couldn't afford to. It was as simple as that. She had to accept this final humiliation at his hands.

Every inch of her skin seemed to burn as she bent to pick up the note. Then, head bent, she went swiftly past him and out into the darkness. And heard the door slam behind her...

There were tears on her face. Phoebe lifted her hands and wiped them angrily away. She hadn't cried then, so why was she allowing herself this weakness now?

She supposed she must be weeping for her lost innocence. For the sheer cruelty of the betrayal she'd been subjected to.

She remembered little of her journey back to the Bishops' house, except that the cab driver had been an older man who'd treated her with a mixture of kindness and disapproval, even offering her a rug to wrap round her.

She'd been miserably ill for most of the following day, and, when she had emerged from her room, found herself the target of some edged remarks about the stupidity of drinking to excess when you couldn't handle alcohol from Tiffany's mother.

'I'm surprised at you, Phoebe,' she'd been told coldly. 'I thought you had more sense. And, if this is the kind of exploit we can expect, you'd better go home. You're not at all a good influence on Tiffany.'

Phoebe had felt too wretched to mount any kind of defence in the face of this onslaught. She was already in Mrs Bishop's bad books through the ruin of her wig.

Tony, she'd soon discovered, was nowhere to be seen.

'You surely didn't think he really fancied you?' Tiffany said derisively. She was sitting on the bed, watching Phoebe pack. 'He just needed someone for this trick he was going to play on Dominic, and you were so obviously smitten, you made it easy for him.'

'Why did he do it?'

It hurt to ask. Her head ached terribly, and she felt as if she'd been kicked in the stomach, but that was nothing to the inner pain—the knowledge that people she'd trusted had degraded her, made a fool of her. Allowed a stranger to badmouth and humiliate her.

Tiffany shrugged. 'They've never liked each other, and Dominic was having this really stuffy birthday dinner with some boring old schoolfriends, so Tony thought he'd liven it up for him. Simple as that.'

She giggled. 'When we all cleared off, he left this note for him to find—"Many happy returns. Your birthday present is unwrapped on your bed". We only wished we could have been there to see his face when he found you. Or yours, when you saw him,' she added spitefully.

She shook her head. 'God, you're so gullible, Phoebe. You must be the only person in the world not to guess there was vodka in that orange juice.'

'Yes,' Phoebe agreed colourlessly. 'Gullible is the word.'

Tiffany eyed her speculatively. 'Tell me, did old

Dom—you know—try anything on? Or were you too far gone to notice?'

'No. Fortunately, he didn't seem to be any more interested in me than Tony was.' Phoebe looked her straight in the eye, and it was Tiffany who lowered her gaze uncomfortably.

'A word of warning,' Tiffany said, after a pause. 'Don't go whingeing to anyone about all this. Because it's our word against yours, and my parents believe that you were so far gone that you passed out and we had to leave you behind. I'm sure you don't want that to be spread about.'

'No,' Phoebe said quietly. 'I wouldn't want that. I suggest we forget the whole thing.'

Tiffany looked frankly relieved. 'I knew you'd see sense. And you should be grateful to us,' she added as she swung herself off the bed and walked to the door. 'At least you won't be so bloody naive in future.'

'I'll bear it in mind,' Phoebe told her retreating back with irony.

She'd never managed the gratitude, but she'd done her damnedest to forget the whole sorry incident. To pretend that it was just one of those things. That she'd healed without scarring.

The fact that Tiffany hadn't returned to school in September, but had moved out to Spain with her parents, had helped.

But she hadn't bargained for the dreams, which had begun a few months later. And, the worse they had got, the more she'd tried to bury the cause of them in her subconscious, she realised now. She'd been afraid to examine what had happened. To confront the bitter truth and defeat it. And this had been compounded by her own lack of anyone to confide in. Not that she could have borne to confess what a fool she'd been.

She'd been young and vulnerable, and she'd been

treated without mercy by Tony and without compassion by Dominic Ashton.

His birthday present, she thought with a flash of anger. Unwrapped on his bed. And she paused.

He was married then, she thought. And if Serena Vane had been with him when he found me, it could have led to all kinds of problems. It was worse than a practical joke. It was real malice.

But his marriage broke down, anyway. And I've carried my problems like a festering sore all this time. But now I've faced up to it, let the poison out.

Impossible as it seems, maybe meeting Dominic Ashton like this has been a kind of therapy. Not, of course, that I ever want to see him again, she amended hastily.

She stood up. Tonight, she thought, I shall sleep without dreaming.

'I'm so sorry, dear.' Mrs Preston's pleasant face was wrinkled with anxiety. 'But I did say it was only a temporary job...'

Phoebe smiled at her. 'Yes, you did, and I understood that, and it's quite all right,' she reassured her. 'I'm glad Debbie's better,' she added, without total sincerity, trying to ignore Lynn pulling hideous faces in the background.

'And I wouldn't want you to leave right away,' Mrs Preston made clear. 'Poor Debbie hasn't regained all her strength yet, so she'll have to ease her way in.'

'Ease is right,' Lynn muttered, when their employer had gone fussing off. 'I don't know why she doesn't put a bed in the kitchen for her.'

Phoebe grinned, and went off to lay the tables for lunch.

For someone who was now virtually redundant, she felt remarkably cheerful. She would hand in her notice to Hanson the Hateful at the end of the week. Then, as soon as Mrs Preston released her, she could leave Westcombe. After that—the world was her oyster.

It wasn't the most pleasant of days—cold, with squally showers driven by a biting wind—and the tea rooms weren't particularly busy.

Phoebe was warming herself with a cup of tea when the bell tinkled, signalling the arrival of a customer.

'Your table,' Lynn commented, peeping through the round window in the kitchen door. 'You lucky devil.'

'Very funny.' Phoebe gulped down the rest of her tea, and picked up her order pad.

'I'm not kidding.' Lynn rolled her eyes. 'He's gorgeous in a brooding way.'

'Let me see.' Phoebe craned her neck, then stepped back, aware that all the colour had drained out of her face. She tried to sound casual. 'You think he's so lovely—you have him. I'll swap tables with you.'

'You're on,' said Lynn instantly. But she was back within a minute. 'What's going on, Phoebe? He's asked for you. Do you know him?'

Phoebe bit her lip, cursing under her breath. 'Our paths have crossed,' she admitted. 'I didn't particularly want to repeat the experience.'

'But he clearly does.' Lynn patted her back. 'Off you go, ducky, and put in a good word for me.'

Dominic Ashton was sitting glancing through the menu as Phoebe approached. He inclined his head formally. 'Hello again, Miss Grant.'

'Just what do you hope to gain from this, Mr Ashton?' she asked in a furious whisper.

'In the first instance, some lunch,' he returned calmly. 'Do you recommend the macaroni cheese?'

'All our food is good,' she told him icily. 'The macaroni cheese comes with a side salad and granary bread. I meant, why did you ask for me?'

'I have an invitation from Tara,' he said. 'She'd like you to come to supper tonight.'

'I'm afraid that isn't possible.' Phoebe wrote down his order. 'Can I bring you something to drink?'

'A pot of coffee—Colombian. And what's so impossible about it? You did go out of your way to befriend the child, after all.'

Yes, she thought, but that was before I knew she was your daughter.

She said shortly, 'I'm busy tonight.'

He gave her a sardonic smile. 'Don't tell me. You have to wash your hair.'

'Oh,' said Phoebe, somewhat nettled. 'Does it look as if it needs it?'

'Not at all, but that is the all-purpose excuse.' He leaned back in his chair, the grey eyes speculative. 'Would it make any difference if I told you I won't be there?'

'No,' she said. 'It wouldn't. I—I just think it's better for me not to see Tara again.'

'Better for whom? Certainly not for Tara. As far as she's concerned, you promised her, and that's sacrosanct.' He paused, then continued levelly, 'As I told you, we only came down here a short while ago, and Tara is finding it hard to settle and make new friends at school. Without Cindy, she's lonely.'

'That's emotional blackmail,' Phoebe said angrily.

'It's also the truth. But, if you can't spare her a couple of hours, there's no more to be said.'

She hesitated. 'And you definitely won't be there?'

'I'm having dinner with Miss Sinclair.'

She sighed. 'All right, then. I'll come over straight from work.'

'No,' he said. 'We'll collect you.' And as her lips parted in protest he went on, 'Tara insists on it.'

Phoebe had the feeling she'd been totally outmanoeuvred, but there was nothing she could do about it.

I'll pay this one visit, she decided as she retreated to

the kitchen, but it will be the first and last. I won't make any more rash promises.

Lynn was agog. 'Who is he?'

'He's that little girl's father,' Phoebe admitted reluctantly. 'I met him when I took her home the other night.'

Lynn nudged her. 'Perhaps he wants to give you a reward.'

Phoebe shook her head. 'It's Tara. She's asked me to have supper with her.'

'And Daddy makes three?'

'No, thank God. He's having dinner with a woman called Hazel Sinclair.'

Lynn looked disappointed. 'That's poor timing.'

'Not from my viewpoint.' Phoebe gave her a faint smile. 'Mr Ashton and I will never be friends.'

'Who mentioned friendship?' asked Lynn.

From then on they were kept too busy for any further discussion, to Phoebe's secret relief.

Dominic Ashton ate his lunch with apparent appreciation and left a generous tip with his bill. Phoebe, her throat tightening, put the money straight into Lynn's jar.

Almost before she knew it, closing time arrived. In the staff cloakroom, Phoebe washed her face and hands then released her hair from its elastic band, combing it into the smooth bob she wore outside working hours. She applied a discreet touch of colour to her mouth, studying herself doubtfully in the mirror.

The door opened and Lynn flew in to collect her coat.

'Your escort awaits,' she announced. 'Nice to see you tarting yourself up for once,' she added approvingly, and fled.

Tarting myself up? Phoebe thought in utter dismay. Oh, God. Not down that path again.

She scooped her hair back, securing it firmly at the nape of her neck again, and scrubbed at her lips with a tissue. Then she put on her coat, picked up her bag and walked sedately out into the café.

'Out for the evening, dear?' asked Mrs Preston, who'd arrived to cash up. 'Have a lovely time.'

Phoebe returned her smile with a certain constraint. Dominic Ashton was waiting at the door, Tara bouncing beside him.

She's too pleased to see me, Phoebe thought, aware that her own heart had lifted involuntarily in response to the little girl's beaming smile. These are deep waters I'm getting into.

Tara tucked a hand into hers. 'We're having special shepherd's pie, and marmalade pudding,' she confided.

Phoebe laughed. 'I can hardly wait.'

'And I helped lay the table. We're having candles, just like Daddy.'

'I've got a reservation at the Clair de Lune,' Dominic explained. 'Apparently it's hot on atmosphere. I'll reserve judgement about the food.'

'It has a good reputation,' Phoebe returned stiltedly. She didn't particularly want to hear, she discovered, what arrangements he'd made for a romantic dinner *à deux*.

But he's divorced, she thought with a mental shrug. He's entitled. I could probably be heading for a candlelit dinner myself, if I didn't freeze off every man who comes near me.

She gave him a swift sideways glance as they went out to the Range Rover. He was wearing tailored charcoal trousers with a matching roll-neck sweater topped by an elegant cashmere jacket. There was no denying his unstudied attraction, she realised with a sudden pang. And swiftly turned her undivided attention to his daughter—where it should have been in the first place, she reminded herself tersely.

Tara chatted happily about school—how many sums she'd got right, the page she'd reached in her reading book—but it was all about lessons, Phoebe noted rather soberly. She didn't mention other children at all.

She was concentrating so hard on what Tara was saying about the hamster who lived in her classroom that she missed the lurch of apprehension in the pit of her stomach as they turned in at the gate.

'Oh,' said Tara in surprise, peering at the car parked outside the house. 'We've got a visitor.'

Carrie opened the door for them, looking rather po-faced. 'Miss Sinclair is here, sir. She's waiting in the drawing room.'

Hazel Sinclair was standing by the fire, one slim foot on the brass fender, gazing pensively into the flames. She wore a pleated skirt in ice-blue georgette with a matching tunic top, and her blonde hair was wound into a smooth coil on top of her head.

Nicely posed, thought Phoebe, and chided herself for being bitchy.

Hazel turned smilingly at their entry. 'Dominic, darling. Yes, I know you were supposed to be picking me up at my house, but I got your message that you might be slightly delayed, and Mummy wanted me to do an errand for her in the village—some crisis over the parish magazine—so here I am instead.' Her blue gaze travelled past him and sharpened slightly. 'Good evening, Tara. Good evening, Miss er...?'

'Grant,' said Phoebe.

'Of course.' She gave a little trill of laughter. 'Are we eating here, then?'

'No.' Dominic's brows lifted. 'I've booked a table at the Clair de Lune. Why do you ask?'

She shrugged elegantly. 'I thought perhaps Miss Grant was here to help Carrie wait at table.'

'Unfortunately not,' Phoebe said affably, thinking of the pleasure of tipping hot soup into that pastel georgette lap.

'Phoebe's having supper with me,' Tara put in unsmilingly.

'Oh, dear.' That laugh again set Phoebe's teeth on

edge. 'Have I committed a *faux pas*? Actually, it was Carrie I was thinking of. She seemed to be limping when I arrived, and I was concerned about her arthritis.'

'Carrie claims she's as fit as a flea,' Dominic said rather shortly. 'And she doesn't take kindly to alternative suggestions.'

Hazel dropped a mock curtsy. 'Then my lips are sealed.'

Oh, that they were, thought Phoebe. Preferably with superglue.

Aloud, she said to Tara, 'Come on, chicken, let's go and find our supper, shall we?'

As they left the room she heard Hazel say in a low voice, 'Dominic, I don't wish to interfere, but do you really think…?'

Tara was scowling as they went upstairs. 'I don't like her. Bridget Thomson says her mummy says that she's going to be my new mummy, and I don't want her to be.'

'On the other hand, you don't want your father to live on his own,' Phoebe suggested fairly.

'He's not alone,' Tara said indignantly. 'He's got me.'

'Yes, but you're usually in bed by seven-thirty, which means he has no one to talk to all evening.'

'Bridget's mummy says they used to go out together a long time ago and she's hoping for better luck this time.'

Bridget's mummy, thought Phoebe, should learn to mind her own business.

All the same, she found herself wondering if the rumour was true. Could he really be planning to marry that obnoxious woman?

And if he is, she thought, startled, why on earth should it concern me?

And to that question, disturbingly, she could find no satisfactory answer at all.

CHAPTER FIVE

THE shepherd's pie was succulent, with minced lamb and vegetables in a rich gravy, and the marmalade pudding with its vanilla sauce melted in the mouth. Phoebe's praise was warm when Carrie came to clear the table, and she saw the rather austere face soften.

'Just nursery food, miss, but nice to have it appreciated. That Cindy never wanted anything but steak,' she added with a snort.

'May I help carry things down to the kitchen?' Phoebe asked diplomatically.

'Bless you, there's no need. There's a dumb waiter in the kitchenette, which saves all that toiling up and down with trays. Mr Dominic's mother had it put in.'

'Oh.' Phoebe followed, and helped load the dirty crockery. 'Is she still alive?'

'No, miss, nor his father either,' Carrie said regretfully. 'But his stepmother's still with us,' she added in a tone she tried too hard to keep neutral. 'At least, she's in Bermuda with her third husband. A gentleman given to sailing, I understand.'

Phoebe's lip twitched. 'Then he's chosen the right place,' she said gravely.

'And a fair distance away, too,' Carrie muttered. 'I just hope she stays there.'

'Did—Mr Dominic get on with her?'

'He did his best, for his father's sake. But she was a lady that was all for herself—and that pesky son of hers. For a couple of years, after his father died, Mr Dominic never came near this house. She liked to entertain a lot, did Mrs Ashton, and it didn't seem like his home any more.

'When he married, of course, I hoped he'd settle here. But Miss Vane preferred London, because of her work.' Carrie sighed faintly. 'It's a house that needs a family in it, and that's the truth.'

'Well, now it has Tara,' Phoebe said gently.

'Yes.' Carrie gave the nursery door a guarded look. 'But for how much longer? Miss Vane allowed Mr Dominic to have custody of the child because it suited her at the time, but he hasn't heard the last of her by a long chalk.' She shook her head. 'Oh, no. And that Cindy has caused him more problems.'

'Is she out of hospital?'

'Yes, and nicely set up in her boyfriend's flat,' Carrie said darkly. 'She needs her ears boxing, if you ask me. Mr Dominic's been ringing all the agencies trying to find another nanny, but they all say the same—there's no hope of finding anyone suitable until the New Year. And what's to happen in between?'

Her lips thinned. 'Miss Sinclair, of course, wants him to place the child as a weekly boarder at that school she goes to.'

'But she's far too young,' said Phoebe, appalled.

Carrie wagged her head philosophically. 'Well, they seem to take them practically from the cradle—mostly for people who have to work abroad.'

'But that isn't the case with Tara. Oh, you must be wrong.'

'Well, it's bound to be a worry for him. His work takes him away sometimes, and I'm not as young as I used to be—though I'm not quite as past it as some would say,' she added grimly. 'And he has to make sure the little one's properly cared for otherwise his ex-wife might start proceedings to take her back.'

'I'm sure things will work themselves out,' Phoebe said, with no real conviction that they would. Nor could she believe she was actually standing here discussing details of Dominic Ashton's private life, and future plans, with his housekeeper.

I'm not interested, she argued with herself. And quite definitely not involved.

She forced a smile. 'In the meantime, I'd better play Snakes and Ladders with Tara while I have the chance.'

When Phoebe returned to the nursery, Tara said severely, 'You've been a very long time. I'm going to have the red counter. You can be blue.'

'Fine by me.' Phoebe sat down beside her at the big square table, and the game began.

Like most young children, Tara was far keener to climb the ladders than she was to slide down the snakes, and there were a few jutting lips and sullen expressions before the game came to an end. On the other hand she was quick to spot a little judicious cheating on Phoebe's part to help her win, and told her to stop or it wouldn't be fair.

When the game was over, Phoebe found a pack of cards, and they played a couple of uproarious games of Snap and a quieter hand of Beggar My Neighbour.

After which, Carrie appeared in the doorway. 'Time for your bath, Tara.'

The little girl pouted mutinously. 'No, I don't want a bath. I want another game.'

'Well, you certainly won't have one if you're going to behave like that,' Phoebe said sternly. 'It's already well past your bedtime, and there's school tomorrow.'

'I hate school. I want to stay up till Daddy comes.' Tara banged her hand on the table.

'Temper,' said Carrie, shocked.

Phoebe leaned forward. 'Listen, poppet. If Daddy finds you're not in bed when he comes back, he'll be angry with Carrie and with me. And he'll never let me come back to play games with you again.' My God, she thought. What am I saying? 'So you have to choose.'

Tara gave her a long look. 'Will you come back and play tomorrow?'

'I can't promise that. But it will be soon. Only you must have your bath now, and go to bed.'

'When I'm in bed, will you read me a story?' Tara wheedled.

'Just one,' Phoebe said severely.

'The one about Winnie the Pooh and the Heffalump?' Tara asked hopefully. 'The book's on my special shelf.'

Phoebe smiled at her. 'Mine, too.'

In the end, seeing how stiffly Carrie bent to turn off the taps, she found herself joining in with Tara's bathtime too. It was a wet and messy affair, featuring a green-spotted rubber frog which leapt out of the water after being firmly held down, showering everyone within range.

'And just who is supposed to be the grown-up out of the pair of you?' Carrie enquired with mock severity.

Phoebe calmed proceedings down by showing Tara how to lather her hands and blow wobbly, multicoloured bubbles through her fingers.

'That was the best bathtime ever,' Tara told her solemnly as Carrie enveloped her in a big towel. 'Cindy always used to say "Hurriupforcrysake".'

'Well, I expect she had a lot of work to do after you were in bed,' Phoebe returned noncommittally. This nanny business, she thought uneasily, is a minefield.

'One story,' she said, finding the place in the book. 'Then you must go to sleep.'

Tara shook her head. 'I have to wait for Daddy to say good night to me.'

Phoebe bit her lip. 'The thing is, chicken, Daddy's gone out for the evening, and may not be back until very late.'

'Why?'

'Because when you're having fun you don't always want to come home straight away. You know that.'

'But Daddy knows I wait for him.'

'Yes,' Phoebe agreed carefully, 'and that's marvellous for him. But he does have a life that isn't—just in this house with you.'

'Doesn't he want me?' It was the most desolate question Phoebe had ever heard. She put a gentle arm round the little figure.

'Of course he does.'

'Mummy didn't want me,' Tara said woefully. 'Bridget's mummy said so.'

Phoebe's hands fastened, in her imagination, round the throat of Bridget's mummy.

'And I heard Cindy say,' went on the little voice, 'that Mummy had to choose between me and a man she was seeing, and she chose him.'

Phoebe found herself at a loss for words. 'I'm sure it wasn't that simple,' she managed eventually.

There was a silence. Then Tara added, 'What will happen if a lady that Daddy's seeing says he has to choose, and he picks her instead of me?'

'That,' Phoebe said steadily, 'will not happen. Because your father's already made his choice, and nothing will change that.'

'How do you know?'

'Because he loves you, and he would never break his word to someone he loved.' Phoebe could hardly believe she'd just said that. That she was actually defending Dominic Ashton, the monster who'd ruined six years of her life.

She took a breath. 'You see, he decided, with your mother, that it would be better for you to stay here than go to Hollywood. And that's all there is to it.'

'I'd have liked Hollywood,' Tara said indignantly. 'Mummy said I'd be called Tara Vane, and she'd get me a part in a film. And I could have my ears pierced,' she added with a sigh.

In spite of her concern, Phoebe felt her lips twitch.

'Well, I expect Daddy will let you too—in about ten years' time. Now, am I going to read you this story?'

'Ooh, yes.' Tara wriggled down in the bed.

Phoebe kept her voice deliberately low, and, gradually, the magic that a man had created for his own small son seventy years ago had its special effect. Before Pooh and Piglet had discovered the truth about Heffalumps, Tara's eyelids were drowsy. And as the story ended she was on the edge of sleep.

As Phoebe gently shut the book a small hand reached out and took hers.

'Don't go,' Tara murmured, and her eyes closed.

This, Phoebe thought fiercely, staring into space, just isn't fair. I don't need it. Any of it.

But she stayed where she was, all the same, watching the child's relaxed face and listening to her quiet breathing.

From the corner of her eye, she was aware of the faintest of movements from the doorway. Without turning, she said softly, 'Carrie, have you come to take over?'

'It's not Carrie.'

Phoebe's heart thudded violently as she heard the amused note in the deep voice, and she twisted in her chair, her face a picture of disbelief.

'You're back already? But you can't be.'

'Then I'm a mirage,' he said equably, treading quietly across the carpet.

Phoebe, against her will, saw the dark face soften into disarming tenderness as he bent to drop a kiss on Tara's tumbled curls. Another intimate insight she could have done without, she reflected bitterly.

'I think you can leave your post.' The smile was transferred to Phoebe. 'Carrie says you're wonderful with her, which is praise indeed.'

'It's not difficult.' Phoebe preceded him to the door,

crossly aware that her breathing was flurried. 'She's a very lovable child.'

'In spite of her parents?' he added silkily. 'Wasn't that the inevitable rider?'

Phoebe didn't look at him. 'That's really none of my business.'

'Rubbish.' Dominic closed the night-nursery door with care. 'You obviously have very strong views. I can sense them seething behind that straight face of yours like a log-jam.'

'Very well,' said Phoebe, nettled. 'I think Tara feels chronically insecure.'

'Since Cindy went?'

'Before Cindy ever came,' she said impatiently. 'Tara deserves better than a succession of professional staff who are just passing through, however qualified they may be. She needs a—a permanent influence in her life. Someone to give her emotional stability.' She paused, flicking a glance at his enigmatic face. 'You did ask,' she added defensively.

'Yes, I did.' He paused. 'Actually, I agree with you, and I've made it my current priority.'

Hazel Sinclair, I suppose, Phoebe thought, feeling oddly dejected. And how will Tara react to that?

She said sedately, 'I—I hope you had a pleasant evening.'

'You mentioned the restaurant's reputation,' he returned, his mouth twisting. 'It's been living on it for some time, at a guess. The pudding, at least, was edible, so we decided to quit while we were ahead and come back here for coffee.'

'Oh,' she said, rather blankly. 'Then I'll get out of your way.'

'No,' he said. 'You'll have coffee with us, then I'll run you home.'

'But Miss Sinclair...'

'Brought her own car, remember? Any more objections?'

Plenty, she thought, in which I shall probably be joined by Miss Sinclair.

Hazel's smile was glittering as they entered the drawing room. 'What amazing devotion to duty,' she drawled. 'I can see you're bent on becoming a family treasure.'

'On the contrary,' Phoebe walked to one of the sofas which flanked the wide fireplace and sat down. 'In the New Year, I shall be looking for a job in my own profession.'

'More waitressing?' Hazel's eyebrows rose.

'No,' Phoebe said levelly. 'I'm sorry to shatter your illusions, but I'm a qualified librarian.'

'Ah,' Dominic said quietly, as if some unspoken question of his own had been answered.

'Then why on earth waste your time in some potty little café?' Hazel demanded.

Dominic looked at Phoebe with an odd smile. 'Because she doesn't see it like that. She's with people she likes in pleasant surroundings—right, Miss Grant?'

'Perfectly correct.' Phoebe was relieved to see Carrie coming in with the coffee-tray. It was disturbing to realise what close attention Dominic Ashton must have paid to their conversation the other night.

But he was not to be allowed a similar opportunity this evening. As they drank their coffee Hazel switched the focus to herself and kept it there, switching from playful, almost girlish chatter to adroitly handled affectionate reminiscence and back again.

A skilful performance, Phoebe decided judiciously. If she's not quite sure of him yet, she means to be. And she gave a little sigh which she hastily turned into a smothered yawn as Dominic turned to look at her.

'Tired, Miss Grant?'

'Oh, no,' Phoebe lied quickly, aware of a less than

playful glance from Hazel. 'Please don't break up the party on my account.'

'I think I'm going to have to. I have a big day tomorrow.' He smiled at Hazel. 'I did explain.'

'Darling, I totally understand. Such a pity you have to drive all the way to Westcombe and back first.' She put a red-tipped hand on his arm and smiled into his eyes. 'Never mind; next time I'll cook for you, sweetie, and we'll make sure we have the whole evening to ourselves. Now, walk me to my car—if Miss Grant will excuse us, of course?' she added sweetly.

'With pleasure,' said Phoebe in equally honeyed tones, and with considerably more sincerity.

When Dominic returned, some ten minutes later, he was putting his handkerchief back in his pocket.

Wiping off the lipstick, thought Phoebe, strongly tempted to say, You missed a bit.

'Ready, Miss Grant?'

He sounded a trifle curt, which was understandable, she conceded, under the circumstances. He'd had a lousy but expensive meal, and her presence had fouled up the after-dinner entertainment.

On the other hand, he'd had an unpaid babysitter, and she hadn't asked him to take her home. And Hazel Sinclair was undoubtedly a bitch.

An imp of pure malice stirred within her.

'I'm glad I wasn't after the job of family treasure,' she remarked pensively as they drove through the starlit lanes. 'I think it's been taken.'

'Miss Sinclair,' he said icily, 'is a very old friend.'

'But so well preserved,' said Phoebe brightly.

There was a silence. 'Are you always so rude about comparative strangers?' he asked with dangerous calm.

'Invariably,' said Phoebe, not giving a hoot.

To her surprise, an unwilling laugh was forced from him. 'Were you ever spanked as a child?'

'Lots of times, but probably not enough to suit you, Mr Ashton.'

'You took the words out of my mouth,' he murmured.

The Range Rover turned sharply to the left, and Phoebe sat up. 'You've taken the wrong turning. Westcombe's the other way.'

'We're not going straight there. We're going to the Green Man in Cottring for a drink.'

Phoebe's lips parted in an outraged gasp. 'I don't want a drink. What the hell is this?'

Dominic sighed impatiently. 'Then stay thirsty,' he said. 'Watch me drink instead. It's not important. There's something I want to talk to you about.'

'Why can't we talk now—on the way home?'

'Because I need to concentrate on driving and serious conversation gets in the way.' He paused. 'Can you drive, by the way?'

'Yes. My father gave me lessons for my seventeenth birthday.' She gave him a suspicious look. 'Why?'

He shrugged a shoulder. 'It's fairly essential these days, especially in country districts.'

'Then it won't really matter to me,' she said rather flatly. 'It's almost certain any library posts going will be in cities.'

'Is that what you want?'

She gave a wintry little smile. 'It's more a question of necessity. I've been marking time—since my father... But it can't go on indefinitely. I've got to strike out. Make a life for myself.' She swallowed. 'New year—new start.'

'We'll drink to it,' he said, and pulled into the Green Man's car park.

It was a whitewashed, timbered building reputedly dating back to mediaeval times. Dominic led the way into the lounge, which was furnished in traditional style, with high-backed settles and heavy wooden tables. There was an inglenook fireplace occupied by a large, wood-burning stove, which gave out a pleasant heat. On top of the log basket, which stood beside it, a large black and white cat was fast asleep. Apart from the cat, they had the room to themselves, although there was a hum of voices and laughter from the public bar next door.

'It's very quiet.' Phoebe sat down near the stove.

'It's skittles night—the one night they don't do food,' he explained. 'Otherwise you wouldn't get a table.' He paused. 'What can I get you to drink?'

Phoebe hesitated. 'Just a tonic water, please.'

His brows lifted in faint mockery. 'Nothing stronger? You might need it.'

Phoebe's heart skipped a beat. 'I'll take my chances.' She tried to speak lightly, but she felt thoroughly uneasy.

What on earth was he going to say to her? she wondered frantically as the landlord came through from the other bar to take their order. Had he—oh, God—suddenly remembered her after all? Recalled the circumstances of their first meeting? Oh, no, she wailed inwardly. Please, no.

He came back with her tonic and a glass of bitter for himself.

He said without preamble, 'You still don't think much of me, do you, Phoebe?'

She stiffened. 'I don't know what you mean.'

'Oh, don't play games. You wear your hostility like armour plating.' He was silent for a moment. 'But, despite what you may think, I do have Tara's best interests very much at heart.'

Phoebe took a gulp of tonic. 'I—I do know that.'

'But it doesn't make you like me any better.' It was a statement, not a question. 'Well, I can live with that. The question is—can you?'

She shook her head. 'You've lost me, I'm afraid, Mr Ashton.'

'Dominic,' he said. 'My name is Dominic, and I'd like you to use it.'

'There's really no point,' she objected, startled. 'We probably shan't be seeing each other again.'

'But I hope we will.' He stared down at his glass. 'The other night Tara suggested you should become her nanny. I said you probably had a hundred reasons to refuse.'

'Yes,' she said. She could feel herself beginning to tremble. 'I have. I told Tara—'

'I know,' he interrupted gently. 'All the same, I'm asking you to forget them all, including your dislike of me, and think of her instead.'

He reached out and covered her hand with his. 'I want you to come and look after her for me, Phoebe. Just until the New Year, when I can make some more permanent arrangement and you can get on with your life.'

He paused. 'Well, what do you say?'

CHAPTER SIX

PHOEBE stared at him for a long moment in utter silence. Then, recollecting herself, she snatched her hand away.

'No,' she said. And again, 'No. It's not possible.'

'Why not?'

'For one thing, I'm not a nanny. I'm totally unqualified to look after a child.'

'Is that all?'

'I'd have said it was enough.'

He shook his head. 'Not for me. You'll have to do better than that.'

'I already have a job—in which I'm very happy.'

'Not for much longer. I had a chat with your Mrs Preston while I was having lunch today, and she told me all about her niece coming back, and how sorry she was to have to let you go. So there's no problem there.'

She said rigidly, 'How dare you discuss me like that—behind my back? How bloody dare you?'

'You'll find I dare quite a lot, especially where Tara's well-being is concerned.' The grey eyes met hers very calmly and directly. 'I'm waiting for the next excuse.'

'Fine.' She drew a breath. 'It simply wouldn't work, and we both know it. You—you don't know anything about me—not really.'

'I'm making discoveries all the time, and expect to make more. I know you have a warm heart, and courage too, even if it does run away with your tongue at times. I know you like my daughter and care about her. And, more importantly, I trust Tara's instinct where you're concerned.'

'Oh, you have it all worked out,' she said bitterly. 'I suppose this is where I dissolve into grateful tears.'

'If you dissolved into anything, you little shrew, I'd expect it to be sulphuric acid,' he said amiably. 'Think about it. I'm talking six to seven weeks at the very outside. Surely you can tolerate me for that long? For Tara's sake?'

'It's precisely for her sake that I can't do this,' she said. 'I've told you already she doesn't need an endless procession of people passing through her life.'

She paused. 'She needs one—special person, who's going to be there always.' She swallowed, aware that her heart was pounding. 'Not a nanny—a mother.'

'She had one, once.' He spoke with a kind of harsh flippancy. 'It didn't work out. But I take your point. And, as I mentioned, I'm working on that very problem at the moment. But—these things take time. After all, I've made one serious mistake already. This time I'm going to get it right.'

Not, something inside her cried out, if you're going to marry Hazel Sinclair. You'll be out of the frying pan and into the fire. You can't do it.

She drew a quick, sharp breath which hurt. This was dangerous thinking. Dominic Ashton's choice of a woman had nothing to do with her. It was not something she could afford to care about. So she stayed mute.

'And, when I do marry again, it won't be simply to provide Tara with a mother either,' he went on. 'Condemn me for selfishness, if you like, but I want a wife first and foremost.'

'That's—natural.' Phoebe tried to relieve the nagging ache in her throat with a sip of her tonic.

'But, in the meantime, Tara needs care, and I'd like you to give my offer serious consideration. For God's sake, Phoebe, you can't pretend your present situation is ideal. Whatever your long-term plans, you're going to need another job pretty damn soon.'

'I'm aware of that,' she said. 'But I don't need charity.' *Especially from you*, were the unspoken words which seemed to hang in the air between them.

'And I wasn't offering it. All the altruism would be on your side, believe me.' He paused. 'Look—this has obviously been a bit of a shock, and if I've come on too strong then I'm sorry. But we both have problems, and this could be a solution.'

Or the start of the kind of problems I'd never even dreamed of, Phoebe thought unsteadily.

She swallowed. 'I'm sure you mean to be kind...'

'Pragmatic,' he corrected.

'But I'd be entirely the wrong person—for all kinds of reasons.' She finished her drink and stood up. 'And now I'd really like to go home, please.'

'Of course.' There was a new formality in his tone. Her decision, clearly, had been accepted and he was moving on.

But wasn't that exactly what she'd wanted? Phoebe asked herself, feeling unaccountably depressed.

They accomplished the remainder of the journey in a rather taut silence.

As they entered Westcombe Dominic drew in at the side of the road in response to the imperative demand of a siren behind them.

'Trouble for someone,' he remarked as a fire engine surged past.

And in my direction, Phoebe realised, leaning forward to watch its progress with a stab of unease.

Before they got to Rushton Street, the acrid smell of burning was filtering into the Range Rover. Dominic found the way into the street barred by a police car. The driver came up to them. 'Sorry, sir, the road is closed. You'll have to go back. House fire being dealt with.'

'So I see,' Dominic said grimly, staring down the street. 'But you'll have to let us through. The fire is in this lady's house.'

'Is it, now? We understood the owner was a Mr Hanson. He's down there now in a right state.'

Phoebe was sitting rigidly, her eyes fixed on the fire tenders filling the street outside Hawthorn Cottage, the moving figures. The smoke seemed to fill her nose and mouth, choking her.

She said hoarsely, 'I'm the tenant.'

'Sorry to hear that, my love. The lads have got the fire out, but there's been a lot of damage. I reckon the whole place will have to be pulled down.'

Somehow, she found herself walking down the road. Dominic's hand was under her arm, holding her up.

'This is your fault.' Arthur Hanson loomed out of the darkness, his face contorted. 'A spark from that grate of yours. I shall sue you for negligence...'

'I didn't light the fire. I haven't been home.' Her voice shook as she looked up at the blackened masonry and empty windows. At the fallen roof. 'My clothes—my things...'

'My valuable furniture.' Hanson was almost dancing with rage. 'You haven't heard the last of this.'

'And neither have you, Mr Hanson.' The fire officer came up to them. 'From what I've seen, I'd say it was a fault in the electrics. You've been warned about dangerous wiring in other properties of yours.'

'The sitting room light,' Phoebe said numbly.

'Very probable, miss.' He patted her shoulder. 'Be thankful you weren't injured.' He paused. 'We couldn't save much, but one of the lads brought out a tin box. Does that belong to you?'

'Yes.' Phoebe gulped, aware that tears were running down her face. 'It's got my private papers in it. Some photographs...'

He nodded. 'I'll get it for you. Now, have you got somewhere to go tonight?'

'Yes,' said Dominic. 'She has.' His arm was round

her, pinioning her against him. Without it, she thought, she might well have fallen to the ground.

'Then if I could have the address, sir? Because I'll need to talk to the young lady tomorrow. And the insurance company will want to know too.'

'She'll be at North Fitton House at Fitton Magna.'

The quiet words penetrated the tear-dimmed haze around her. She looked up at him, her eyes dilating. She tried to say no, but no sound would come from her dry mouth.

'Don't be a little fool,' he said softly as the fire officer moved away. 'What choice do you have? We'll collect your box and I'll take you home.'

After that everything seemed to dissolve into a blur. The only reality seemed to be the tin box she held on her lap. She could feel the sharp edges pressing into her hands.

She was still clutching it when Dominic led her back into his drawing room and sat her gently down on the sofa. She watched him kick the smouldering logs back to life. Saw Carrie bustle in with a tray of tea, and place it on a table in front of her.

Dominic sat down beside her. 'You can put it down now,' he said. 'It's quite safe.'

She shook her head numbly. 'It's all I have left,' she said. 'Everything in the world. That's quite funny, isn't it? Because it's not a very big box.' And she began to laugh, while the tears splashed down her white face.

From a distance, she heard Carrie say, 'Shock. I'll call Dr Foster.'

Then she felt herself lifted, held close on his lap. Her face was pressed into his shoulder. She breathed the fragrance of clean wool, and the sharper, evocative scent of his skin, so alien in its masculinity, yet somehow so completely, so achingly familiar. And all the time fierce sobs fought their way up from the depths of her being, shaking her whole body.

He was stroking her as if she were a young, frightened animal, his hands gentling her back, coaxing the tense muscles to relax. Smoothing her tangled hair.

'It's all right,' he whispered, repeating the words over and over again like some mantra. 'Everything's going to be all right.'

And, when she could cry no more, she lay in his arms, spent and shivering, watching the dancing flames and thinking how easily she could have been overcome by smoke and trapped in the burning house.

It was only when Carrie brought the doctor in and Phoebe caught her swift, appraising glance that she actually realised that she was still sitting on Dominic's knee.

Face hot, she scrambled awkwardly to her feet, avoiding his eyes.

Dr Foster was kind and matter-of-fact, assuring her that tears were an excellent therapy, and prescribing bed, cocoa and a mild sedative as follow-up treatment.

'And a hot bath first,' added Carrie, ushering her upstairs. 'Everything's ready for you.'

Phoebe sank gratefully into the hot, scented water. She could hardly believe how swiftly and fundamentally her life had changed. She looked round at the immaculately tiled room, at the thick towels warming on their rail, the dark red silk dressing gown waiting to receive her.

It was the kind of luxury she'd avoided over the past few years, and it was undeniably seductive. But she knew she must resist it.

The dressing gown was far too big. She had to roll up the sleeves and wind the sash twice round her slender waist before trailing back into the bedroom. She supposed it must belong to Dominic, and wearing it made her uneasy, but, under the circumstances, she had little choice.

The bed had been turned down, she saw, and the prescribed cocoa was waiting on the night table with the tablets the doctor had left.

Phoebe had just set the beaker down when Carrie came bustling in.

'All gone? That's a good girl,' she approved briskly. 'Now, you have a good sleep, and tomorrow everything will seem much better.'

'Everything's gone, Carrie.' Phoebe settled obediently against the pillows. 'I've been left with the clothes I stand up in. That's something you hear people say, but you never think of it actually happening.'

'Well, don't you worry about it,' Carrie advised comfortably, turning off the light. 'Mr Dominic will take care of everything. You'll see.'

Yes, thought Phoebe, reluctantly composing herself for sleep. That's just what I'm afraid of.

And when she slept she found herself tormented by dreams of Dominic's arms holding her, making her safe, keeping her secure. Only, in the way of dreams, that was strangely no longer enough. And, in the darkness, she felt herself reach out, whispering his name.

When she opened her eyes the next morning, she felt totally disorientated. Then, as she remembered the events of the previous evening, she sank back into the bed again with a faint groan. It wasn't just another bad dream. The cottage had burned down, and she was in Dominic Ashton's house, in one of his rooms, wearing his robe.

Nor, she discovered, was she alone. A small, rather battered teddy bear wearing a blue ribbon was sitting beside her pillow.

Phoebe picked it up, a reluctant smile curving her lips. No need to ask who'd left it there, she thought with a faint twist of the heart. As she replaced it she caught sight of the small gilt clock on the night table and froze.

It was nearly eleven o'clock. Morning coffee at the café had begun almost an hour ago, and she wasn't there.

It must have been those damned tablets, she thought as she hurriedly threw back the covers and swung her feet to the floor. But it was the first time she'd ever been late, and Mrs Preston would surely understand.

In the bathroom doorway, she paused with a yelp of dismay. She'd left her uniform on the floor in the bathroom last night, but it wasn't there now. Someone—presumably Carrie—had removed it.

Well, she'd simply have to find Carrie and get her things back, or she wouldn't be at work in time to serve lunches.

Trying not to trip on the hem of the robe, she went out of the room and trod down the stairs. But she could hear no sound, no sign of life, just as if the sleep she'd woken from had been enchanted and the house was still caught in the spell.

Then, 'Good morning.' Dominic Ashton had appeared silently in his study doorway, and was standing, looking up at her, hands on hips.

'Oh.' Phoebe's hand went to her throat, pulling the edges of the robe together. 'I—I was looking for Carrie, actually.'

'She's gone out. I think she planned to be back before you woke.' He gave her a faint smile. 'The robe suits you. And, in case you were wondering, it's new. I've never worn it.'

'Oh,' was all Phoebe could think of to say, aware that she was blushing.

'Did you sleep well?' he asked.

She bit her lip. 'Rather too well,' she answered, constrained. 'I'm late for work.'

'Actually you're not. I telephoned earlier and explained that you wouldn't be in. Mrs Preston was most sympathetic, and said it would give Debbie a chance to get back in harness.'

The colour in her face deepened angrily. 'You had no business saying anything of the kind. I have my living to earn.'

'Not, I suspect, at the Clover Tea Rooms,' he said calmly. 'But we'll discuss that later. In the meantime, Carrie would want me to offer you breakfast.'

'I'm not hungry,' she snapped.

'Truly?' His smile widened. 'You look to me as if you're ready to take a bite out of something.'

'I'm merely looking for my clothes.'

'Carrie washed them. They won't be dry yet.'

'Oh, no,' Phoebe wailed. 'Then what on earth am I supposed to do?'

'Relax and have some breakfast,' he suggested lazily. 'A day off will do you no harm.'

'Not if I'm out of work at the end of it,' she said resentfully.

'Don't be a pessimist. Your prospects are far better than that.' He paused. 'Tara sends her love, by the way, and says she'll see you after school.'

'Unlikely,' Phoebe said curtly. 'As soon as I get my clothes back, I'm out of here.'

There was a silence, then he asked slowly, 'What are you so afraid of?'

She lifted her chin. 'I'm not scared at all. I—I just feel I've trespassed on your hospitality long enough.'

'Don't tell lies, Phoebe,' he said amiably. 'You're bad at it. Now, come along to the kitchen and I'll make you some coffee.'

She longed to tell him to keep his coffee, but just the thought of it made her mouth water, so she trailed after him to the rear of the house.

The kitchen was a big room, its windows overlooking a small orchard, the trees stripped and bare now. But it contrived to be cosy, with a dark green Aga taking pride of place. The big wooden dresser and fitted cupboards had clearly been around for a long time, but the appliances were all up to the minute.

Phoebe sat at a long, scrubbed table and watched him prepare the percolator. He was obviously very much at home, whistling softly under his breath as he worked.

He opened the refrigerator, sending her a quizzical look. 'Bacon,' he suggested. 'Scrambled eggs—toast?'

For a moment she hesitated, then nodded, with a stilted, 'Thank you.'

The plate he eventually placed in front of her smelled like ambrosia. The bacon was crisp, the eggs creamy and the toast had been cut into fingers. He poured coffee for them both, and sat opposite her.

'You're quite right, of course,' he said, watching her tuck in. 'This is a shameless attempt to curry favour with you.'

Phoebe took an unguarded swallow and nearly choked.

'You really don't play fair, do you?' she said, wiping her eyes on the sleeve of her robe.

'I tend to apply my own rules.' The grey eyes were intent. 'Think about it, Phoebe. Your home has been destroyed, and your job has probably reached its end. So, where will you go when you leave here? And what are you planning to do?'

'I don't know.' Phoebe finished the last delicious crumb and put down her knife and fork. 'But they're my problems, and I'll manage somehow.'

'And you'd rather rot in hell than accept a helping hand from me.'

She looked down at the table. 'That's not true. You gave me a roof last night. I'm—grateful.'

'Then do something for me in return. My offer still stands. I need you to look after Tara. When she found you'd slept here, she was ecstatic.'

Phoebe bit her lip. 'She left her teddy bear on the bed for me.'

'As a welcome present. She's convinced herself that you're here for the duration. Can you really let that prickly pride of yours get in the way? Cindy let her down badly. Are you going to do the same?'

'That's the worst form of emotional blackmail.'

'Not quite.' The grey eyes were glinting with amusement, and something more disturbing, which made her feel oddly weak. 'I need to keep something in reserve.'

He paused. 'I told Tara that if you came with me to collect her from school this afternoon, it meant you were staying.'

He collected the dirty crockery and loaded it into the dishwasher.

'I have to go out now,' he tossed at her over his shoulder. 'But feel free to wander about—get the feel of the place—and we'll talk later.'

'Mr Ashton,' she began.

'Dominic,' he reminded her, pausing in the doorway. His gaze met hers, held it compellingly.

He said quietly, 'It's about six weeks of your life, Phoebe, for a child who needs you. Would it really cost you so much?'

He went, and a moment later Phoebe heard the front door slam behind him.

He was so sure he'd won, she thought furiously. That he'd offered the only viable solution to their mutual problems.

Oh, if she just had her clothes back, she'd be out of here and on the next train to—anywhere, she thought, grinding her teeth.

Or she would if there wasn't Tara to consider. That was the stumbling block, she realised ruefully. Through no fault of her own she was no longer a totally free agent, and she knew it.

She wandered into the drawing room, and stood staring absently through the window. Clouds scudded across the grey sky, and the trees were bending in the bleak wind. It was a cold world out there, and the house seemed to be wrapping itself round her like a cloak. Offering her a protection that was difficult to reject.

Difficult—but not impossible.

All she had to do was tell him the truth, she thought. Remind him of the naked, drunken girl he'd found on his bed six years before, and he'd be rid of her so fast her feet wouldn't touch the ground.

That was the obvious course to take. If she really wanted to leave...

She stopped right there—aware her breathing had quickened. She found she was remembering suddenly the closeness of his arms around her. The way her skin had seemed to bloom under his touch. The warm and unequivocal eroticism of last night's dreaming.

She moved restlessly, feeling her nipples hardening involuntarily under the tantalising brush of the silk against her naked flesh. Imagining his hands moving on her—not simply with kindness, but with desire.

Her whole body shivered, languidly, expectantly.

She raised suddenly heavy lids and saw herself reflected in the window pane. Saw the drowsy, shadowed eyes, the heated flush along her cheekbones, the soft, vulnerable mouth. The face of a stranger, she thought dazedly. A stranger who'd lost touch with reality.

Six weeks of her life was what he'd asked for, and was all that he wanted. No more, no less.

'Would it really cost you so much?' he'd challenged her.

It could do, she thought. It could cost altogether more than I can afford to pay.

Because it had suddenly and unwillingly occurred to her that the price of those six weeks could be her heart and soul.

She was still standing like a statue, trying to come to terms with her moment of truth and failing utterly, when

Carrie returned.

'I've brought you some things, my dear.' Carrie dumped the chainstore bags she was carrying onto one of the sofas. 'I don't suppose they're your taste, but they'll tide you over until you can choose for yourself.'

Peeping into the bags, Phoebe found an assortment of underwear, two pairs of black leggings and a couple of sweaters patterned in jewel colours to wear with them. There was also a swirl of a skirt, checked in grey and pink, and a pink woollen blouse. Another bag revealed socks, tights and some neat black ankle boots. And Carrie had bought basic toiletries too, including a brush and comb.

'But I didn't expect all this!' Phoebe exclaimed almost in dismay.

'Well, you can't drip around in that robe any longer. It doesn't look right.' Carrie loaded the bags into her arms and gave her a gentle push. 'Go and get dressed, and I'll start showing you where everything is.'

'But I'm not staying,' Phoebe said quickly, and then, when she saw the look of open disappointment on the older woman's face, she amended quickly, 'At least—I haven't decided yet—but I don't think...'

'Sometimes,' Carrie said severely, 'people think so much they end up in total confusion.' She paused. 'But if you want to know what I think, then you're just what Miss Tara needs.' She gave Phoebe's strained face a long look. 'And maybe she's what you need, too. It hasn't been all fun just recently for you—admit it.'

No, Phoebe thought as she went upstairs. But that doesn't justify a thing.

She dressed swiftly in leggings and a sweater, combing her hair so that it curved round her face.

She was embarrassed by the care the other woman had clearly taken to choose clothing that would suit her. It had been a long time since she'd possessed anything half as attractive. But how was she going to pay for it? she wondered, biting her lip.

She received an approving nod when she returned downstairs, and was then swept inexorably into a detailed tour of the house.

Phoebe found she was becoming interested, more or less in spite of herself. Apart from the drawing room, which had been crammed with people, she hadn't seen a great deal of the house on her first visit. But, to her relief, Carrie drew the line at showing her the master bedroom, merely pointing out its closed door in passing.

Up in the nursery area, Phoebe was instructed about the care of Tara's clothes and toys, and shown where everything was kept.

'You won't have to do any actual cleaning. Mrs Watson from the village comes three times a week for that. But you'll be expected to keep these rooms tidy,' Carrie told her. 'Miss Tara's not a great one for putting things away, so you'll have to be firm.'

It doesn't matter, Phoebe wanted to yell, because I'm not staying. I've decided, once and for all, that I don't dare. Because, heaven help me, I can't trust myself.

In reality, she said nothing. Just smiled rather wanly and nodded.

Lunch was home-made broth with crusty bread, and fresh fruit to follow. In spite of her emotional turmoil, Phoebe ate everything that was put before her.

She was shown how to operate the dishwasher and the washing machine. Then, under Carrie's critical eye, she dealt with a basket of ironing deftly and neatly, and replaced a missing button on a small dress.

'My, the days are drawing in.' Carrie shook her head as she looked out of the window. 'It'll be quite dark soon, and I've left a few things on the line in the orchard. Bring them in for me, there's a good girl.'

The strong wind had twisted most of the garments

round the washing line, and it nipped at Phoebe as she struggled to free them.

Above its shrill whine, she heard Dominic quietly say, 'Phoebe.'

She dropped the final pair of Tara's woollen tights into the clothes basket and turned slowly to face him. She hadn't heard his approach over the damp grass, but, even before he'd spoken, she'd felt a sharp ripple of awareness—was conscious that her mouth had already begun to curve into a smile, which she had to hastily wipe away.

He was standing a few yards away from her. Even in the fading light, she could see that the dark face looked strained. That his tall figure was tensed—against what? The possibility of rejection?

But that was ridiculous, she thought. He was still the arrogant Dominic Ashton. Still the Dark Lord of a dream that could so easily develop into yet another nightmare.

A man to avoid. To evade. And soon.

He said simply, 'I'm going to collect Tara from school. Will you come with me?'

And against every instinct, against all reason, Phoebe heard herself say, 'Yes.'

CHAPTER SEVEN

DOMINIC didn't speak. But for a moment Phoebe thought he was going to step forward—reach for her in some way—and every nerve in her body was suddenly tense and tingling.

She swallowed, clutching the basket of clothes as if it were a shield. Because if he touched her she didn't know what she would do. How she would react. And the realisation frightened her, sent her mind spinning.

It was as if she was joined to him by some intense, mutual need that she had never thought to experience, and that she couldn't begin to understand.

He hadn't moved a muscle, but all the same she felt— taken. Stamped for ever by some mark of possession.

Then, as if the invisible cord between them had been slashed with a knife, she was just as suddenly free again, her legs shaking under her, her heart thudding against her ribcage.

He said laconically, 'Get your coat. I'll see you on the front drive in five minutes.' And he turned and went, leaving her staring after him.

After she'd left the clothes basket in the kitchen, explained to Carrie where she was going and fetched her jacket from her room, she had an excuse to be breathless when she joined him on the drive.

He was waiting beside the little Peugeot she'd last seen in the car park beside the market.

'You'll have the use of this while you work for me.' He handed her the keys. 'Let's see what you can do.'

'You want me to drive?' Phoebe gasped.

'You told me you had a licence. I need to check your

general competency if you're going to be driving my daughter.'

'Yes—yes, I see.' She slid behind the wheel, waiting nervously while he took his place beside her. 'It's been a while...'

'Then take your time.'

To her relief, the engine responded immediately, and she moved smoothly away.

'Where exactly are we going?' she asked as she threaded her way through the lanes. She was glad she had to concentrate so hard on what she was doing. It helped divert her attention from Dominic's physical proximity to her in the confined space of the car.

'To Westcombe Park School first, and then into Westcombe itself, where Tara has her piano lesson. Her teacher lives in Derwent Street.'

'Of course.' Phoebe nodded. 'That's just a few doors away from the tea rooms.'

'And probably why Cindy thought she could risk leaving Tara to fend for herself,' he returned flatly.

'Yes—but there was no real harm done.'

He said drily, 'I wish I could agree.'

There was a brief silence, then he continued. 'May I say, by the way, how much I approve of the transformation?'

Phoebe felt her face warm slightly. She said stiltedly, 'I—I have to talk to you about that.'

'That has an ominous sound,' he said lightly. 'Don't you like Carrie's choice for you?'

'That's not the point. I—I don't want anyone else buying my clothes.'

'But your own stuff went up in flames,' Dominic pointed out reasonably. 'And I really couldn't allow you to spend the rest of your life in my robe, however beguiling you looked,' he added silkily.

A remark Phoebe considered it safer to ignore. 'All

the same,' she said stubbornly, 'I wish you hadn't done it. It will take me ages to repay you.'

'Consider it part of the job,' he said dismissively. 'Uniform supplied.'

'This is nothing like a uniform, and you know it.' Phoebe swallowed. 'Please let me have the receipts, and I'll pay for the things as and when I can.'

'Please don't sound as if you'll be going round with a begging bowl,' he said caustically. 'I saw the fire officer today, and he confirmed that the cause of the fire was the faulty wiring, so you probably have a claim against your landlord.'

'I doubt if he'll see it that way.'

'He may not have a choice.' Dominic paused. 'And there is, of course, the question of your salary. We haven't really discussed that yet.'

He mentioned a sum that nearly caused her to stall the car.

'But you can't possibly pay me that much,' she protested. 'I'm not even qualified.'

He said slowly, 'It's what I was paying Cindy. And you have a warm heart and a sense of responsibility—both attributes that she signally lacked. I think you're worth it. That's on top of your board and lodging, of course,' he added, almost as an afterthought.

'Oh, this is ridiculous,' she said heatedly.

'I quite agree. We're going to end up in the ditch.'

'Oh, hell.' Phoebe hurriedly righted her steering. 'You know what I mean.'

'Yes, I do,' he said slowly. 'And I'm wondering why you have such a low sense of self-esteem.'

She bit her lip until she tasted blood. 'I—wasn't aware I had.'

'Another fib,' he said gently. 'You don't trust me enough to tell me the truth. But I can wait.'

You'll wait a long time, she thought wildly. What would you say, I wonder, if I told you that it was all because of you—and only you? Maybe, on the day I leave for ever...

Westcombe Park School was a big square building in red brick. Lights blazed from the windows, and the road outside was busy with Land Rovers and Jeeps while the drivers—mostly women in Barbours and Puffa jackets—called greetings to each other.

Phoebe parked the car neatly and got out, feeling very much an outsider, although she spotted a few girls of her own age who were probably nannies too.

In the distance a bell pealed shrilly, and the children began to emerge from the school building in laughing, chattering groups.

Tara was one of the last to appear, and Phoebe noticed immediately that she was walking on her own, looking down at the ground.

She cupped her hands to her mouth. 'Hi,' she called. 'We're over here.'

The child looked up, and the wistful, slightly withdrawn expression vanished like magic.

'Phoebe.' She hurled herself across the road. 'You're staying. You really are. I wished so hard, and it's come true.'

'Well, I hope you don't regret it.' Phoebe returned her hug. 'I can be a real dragon.'

'Can we go home and play another game?' Tara asked eagerly.

'No, poppet. You have a music lesson, and then your homework to do.' Phoebe decided to get into dragon mode right away.

'Daddy—do I have to go to music?' Tara wheedled.

He pinched her nose gently. 'Yes, my love. Mrs Blake is expecting you.'

'But I want to show Phoebe all my toys.'

'There'll be plenty of time for that.' Phoebe ushered her into the back of the car and fastened her seat-belt.

'You won't go away?' the child asked anxiously. 'People always go away.'

Phoebe felt something twist inside her. 'I'll stay as long as you need me,' she said slowly.

Dominic touched her arm. 'I'd better introduce you to Mrs Franks, Tara's teacher.'

He took her across to a tall woman who'd been standing just inside the school gate, talking vivaciously to a small group of mothers. As she turned away Dominic intercepted her.

'Mrs Franks, this is Phoebe Grant, who will be looking after Tara for me.'

'Another young woman,' Mrs Franks said with a silvery laugh, raking Phoebe with a glance that managed to be inquisitive and dismissive at the same time. 'I do hope for your sake that she's rather more reliable than the last one, Mr Ashton.'

Her voice became earnest. 'You see, we do feel at Westcombe Park that a stable home background is so necessary for the well-being of the individuals in our little community.'

'Yes.' There was a touch of bleakness in Dominic's voice. 'I'm aware of that too.' He turned and strode back to the car. But Phoebe lingered for a moment.

'Is Tara settling in at school?' she asked.

'Naturally.' Mrs Franks bridled a little. 'We pride ourselves on making even the most awkward newcomer feel at home. Why do you ask?'

'It's just that she came out on her own,' Phoebe said rather lamely. 'And I wondered...'

'Isn't it rather soon to be making judgements?' Another tinkle of laughter. 'Generally children of that age find their own level without needing interference from adults.'

'I didn't mean to interfere,' Phoebe said quickly. 'I was just—concerned.'

'And a little over-conscientious, perhaps?' Phoebe

was given a patronising smile. 'I think you can safely leave Tara to us during school hours.' Mrs Franks looked over Phoebe's shoulder. 'Ah, Mrs Dawson, I hoped I'd see you today. It's about Melanie's extra reading...'

Phoebe returned to the car. I probably am worrying for nothing she thought. And yet...

'Shall I come in with you?' Phoebe asked Tara as she parked the car in Derwent Street.

'I don't think she's reached audience standard yet.' Dominic sounded amused. 'We'll go for a stroll while she has her lesson.'

Mrs Blake, Tara's piano teacher, was a tall woman with a calm, humorous face, and Phoebe liked her immediately.

In return she received an appraising look and a firm handshake.

'I'm glad to have seen the last of your predecessor,' she told Phoebe quietly while Tara was finding her music and climbing onto the piano stool. 'Pretending that she'd be there to pick Tara up at my gate, and getting the child to lie for her.' She snorted. 'Unforgivable. She deserves her broken bones.'

Phoebe would have liked to linger in the cosy house, listening to Tara's lesson. The realisation that Dominic was waiting for her was a daunting one. She wasn't sure she wanted to go strolling with him. She seemed to be spending altogether too much time in his company as it was. Hands in pockets, she walked quietly at his side down Derwent Street, and out into the main shopping area.

The High Street had been decorated for Christmas, and a popular DJ from a local radio station had switched on the lights the previous weekend.

Phoebe had spent a miserable Christmas last year and had anticipated a similarly bleak prospect this year. Instead, she'd be able to see Christmas in the only real way—through the eyes of a child, she realised on a small surge of pleasure.

'At last—the glimmer of a smile,' Dominic remarked. 'You've been looking so serious I thought you wanted another of your little talks with me.'

She flushed. 'A lot of things have happened over the past twenty-four hours. You can hardly expect me to be turning cartwheels.'

'But you don't have to look as if you were about to be led out to execution either. Is the thought of caring for Tara really so traumatic?'

'No, of course not,' Phoebe denied, startled. 'She's a darling.'

'And you haven't found evidence that Carrie is practising voodoo in the coalshed?'

A reluctant chuckle escaped her. 'Now you're being absurd.'

'I was afraid of that. In which case, it must be me.' He paused, then said in a very different voice, 'What is it, Phoebe? What have I done?'

All the muscles in her throat tightened. She looked straight ahead of her. 'You've been—very kind,' she said stiltedly. 'Perhaps I just don't respond well to—sudden change.'

'But at least this time it's a change for the better—or should be. Unlike some in the past.' He was silent for a moment. 'And you're still grieving for your father?'

She hesitated. 'Yes. I think I grieve most for the fact that I wasn't there. That he died among strangers.'

'That wasn't your fault. And, though you may not believe me, there are worse fates.'

'What could be worse?'

He said slowly, 'To die knowing that someone you've loved does not love you in return. That you've invested your life—your energy—in worthless stock. That's a terrible loneliness.'

She remembered things Carrie had said, and knew he

was talking of his own father. The passage of time hadn't softened the pain, or the anger.

'When I discovered I'd made the same mistake, I cut my losses immediately,' he went on, almost conversationally. 'I knew that even if I had to be alone for the rest of my life it would be worth it.'

'But you're not alone.' A sudden image of Hazel Sinclair imprinted itself on her mind, and was suppressed. 'You—you have Tara.'

'That,' he said, too gently, 'is not quite the same thing.' He paused. 'And what about you, Phoebe? You're not a child. You've been away to university. There must have been at least one significant other in your life. Maybe more.'

'No one—serious,' Phoebe hedged. No one at all, she thought.

'You mean those barriers of yours aren't just for me? But surely someone must have tried to get close—to solve the enigma?'

'Perhaps they were perceptive enough to realise there wasn't one. That I'm just—'

'An ordinary girl with no secrets?' he supplied drily. 'That's not perception. That's wilful blindness. And I give you due warning, Phoebe Grant—' his voice slowed to a drawl '—that I intend to search you out. To uncover all your secrets—every hidden depth.'

Her whole body seemed to shiver. She stopped dead, turning to stare unseeingly into a shop window festooned with Christmas cheer.

She said in a low voice which vibrated with anger, 'Well, let me warn you in return, Mr Ashton. Taking this job does not mean I'll allow any invasion of my privacy. I'm doing it for Tara—just for Tara. I will not be used for your amusement.'

'Did I give that impression?' he came back swiftly. 'I'm deadly serious.'

'And so am I.' Phoebe swung to face him. 'We are

two separate people, Mr Ashton, who for a short time have to lead parallel lives. But one of the great things about parallels is that they don't meet. And that's the way I want it. For all your generous salary and beautiful home, I won't accept anything else.'

'I see.' He was quiet for a moment. 'Does this stipulation also preclude the friendship I once offered you?'

'You're my employer,' she said. 'I'm your daughter's temporary nanny. That's it. All of it.'

'You're certainly extremely vehement about it,' he commented wryly. 'Which makes me wonder exactly which of us you're most keen to convince.' He left that hanging in the air, and glanced at his watch. 'In the interests of parallelism, I'll see you back at Derwent Street in half an hour.'

Parallelism indeed, Phoebe thought, glaring at his retreating back. I bet there's no such word.

At least she'd drawn the parameters for the next few weeks, she told herself defiantly. And from now on she should be in no danger.

But, in that case, why was she suddenly trembling like a leaf? And why was she peering along the busy street, trying to catch a glimpse of Dominic's tall figure walking away from her?

Fool, she thought angrily, and marched off in the opposite direction.

Tara was in buoyant mood when Phoebe collected her.

'I like Mrs Blake,' she announced, dancing to the car where her father waited silently, his face unreadable. 'I wish she was my teacher for everything.'

'Mrs Franks seems very nice,' Phoebe volunteered mendaciously,

'She has pets,' said Tara. 'And I'm not one.' She climbed into the rear seat. 'Mrs Blake is teaching me a surprise, for Christmas,' she went on gleefully.

'What kind of surprise?' Dominic looked at her, his expression softening.

'If I told you, it wouldn't be a secret any more,' Tara said severely. 'You'll have to wait and see.'

She chattered happily all the way home. As soon as they arrived, Phoebe whisked her up to the nursery to do the small amount of homework the school had set. The child wasn't exactly being stretched by the tasks, Phoebe thought, watching how swiftly and almost offhandedly Tara completed them.

'May I watch television for a bit?' the little girl appealed when she'd finished.

'I don't see why not,' Phoebe conceded, although it occurred to her that she hadn't yet noticed a television set. 'Where do you do that?'

'In the other sitting room—the little one. The piano's there too, so I can do my practising as well,' Tara informed her virtuously.

'Better and better,' Phoebe said drily.

The small sitting room was at the back of the house, and was a homelier version of the drawing room, with faded chintzes and a big sheepskin rug in front of the fireplace, which housed a living-flame gas fire.

With Tara settled raptly in front of a children's programme, Phoebe took the opportunity to look through a glass-fronted bookcase. It contained mostly fiction, some of it dating back to the beginning of the century, but there was a wide selection of modern authors too, with the unashamedly popular rubbing shoulders with the literary.

Phoebe, who envisaged spending most of her time in the safety of her room, thought gloatingly that this book collection could become her personal gold mine.

There was a complete set of Georgette Heyer novels, most of which she'd already read, but it would be good to renew her acquaintance with such an elegant and accomplished writer. Inside the front cover of *Friday's*

Child a bookplate announced that this book was the property of Phyllida Ashton.

'My mother,' Dominic said from behind her.

Phoebe started so violently the book nearly flew out of her hands. She said breathlessly, 'I was going to ask if I might borrow it—not just take it.'

His brows drew together. 'Phoebe, for the time being, this is your home. You don't have to ask permission for every little thing.' He turned to his daughter, his frown deepening. 'What are you watching, Tara?'

'Only *Down Under*,' Tara returned, mentioning a popular soap opera a mite warily.

The cool grey eyes rested on Phoebe. 'Isn't that slightly out of her age group?'

'Everyone in my class watches it,' Tara pouted. 'When they talk about it, I don't know what they mean.'

'All the same I'd prefer you watch something more edifying than Australian soap opera.' There was a slight edge to his voice.

'It's just finishing anyway,' Phoebe put in as the child's face grew more mutinous. 'Right on time for your piano practice,' she added cheerfully.

'And my secret.' Fortunately, Tara was easily deflected from her grievance. 'You and Daddy have got to leave the room,' she ordained grandly.

'I'll call you when supper's ready,' Phoebe promised.

As they walked away they heard the first rather wobbly notes of 'Away in a Manger' coming through the door.

Dominic's face relaxed into a grin. 'Her secret is safe with us,' he said softly. 'I'll be the most surprised man in the county, come Christmas Day.'

As he moved away Phoebe said, 'Could you spare me a moment?'

He paused. 'What's this?' he enquired sardonically. 'More rules and regulations for my future conduct?'

'To a certain extent.' She made herself meet his gaze

squarely. 'I gathered just now you don't approve of Tara's viewing choices, and, by implication, you're critical of me for allowing it.'

His tone was curt. 'I'd have said that was obvious. Do you blame me?'

'I can understand your reservations.' She paused. 'But Tara's the new kid on the block. I think she's having problems settling mid-term in a new school. Something as simple as sharing a television programme with her classmates could give her the leverage she needs. Help her to fit in.'

He was frowning again. 'Are you saying she's unhappy at Westcombe Park?'

'I don't know whether it's as cut and dried as that. I suspect she's not particularly challenged by the work.'

'The school has a very good reputation.'

'So had the Clair de Lune.'

His mouth tightened. 'And Miss Sinclair is on the board of governors.'

'Which makes everything perfect, naturally,' she said tautly. 'Please forget that I said anything.'

She was turning away when he put a hand on her arm. 'Wait—please. I'm not dismissing what you say out of hand. But I'm wondering whether it's a little early for you to be making that kind of judgement.'

She smiled without amusement. 'That's what Mrs Franks said, too.'

His brows lifted. He said bleakly, 'You spoke to her— criticised the school—without consulting me first?'

'No,' she said. 'I simply asked if Tara was all right, and got fobbed off.'

He said glacially, 'She may have thought it was none of your damned business.'

She raised her chin. 'You brought me here because I care—remember? Are you now telling me that you want me to stop?'

'No, of course not,' he said irritably. 'But I didn't

expect quite such immediate involvement, perhaps.' His brief laugh was almost explosive. 'Hell, I don't suppose I knew what to expect.'

Phoebe said quietly, 'I don't know either, but I'm sorry if I spoke out of turn. Good evening, Mr Ashton.'

'Where are you going?'

'Upstairs, to lay the table for our supper.'

'For Tara's supper,' he corrected. 'You dine with me, after she's in bed.'

Phoebe took a deep breath. 'Is that what Cindy did?' she asked, giving him a measuring look.

'No,' he said. 'But she didn't take me to task over my daughter's well-being either. You asked me to spare you a moment. Now I require the same favour in return. Dinner will be at eight o'clock, but I'll be up to say goodnight to Tara first.'

There was a silence, then, 'Very well,' Phoebe said icily.

'And very wise, too,' he said silkily, and left her inwardly raging.

She'd calmed down, at least on the surface, by the time Tara appeared in the nursery. Her supper was a savoury pasta dish, with a baked egg custard to follow, and the child ate every scrap.

When the meal was over, Phoebe taught her to play clock patience until it was time for the child's bath.

'It's such a waste going to bed when I'm not sleepy,' Tara sighed as Phoebe tucked her in. 'Will you read me a story, please? I'd like the one about Snow White.'

'Are you sure? It's a bit scary for bedtime.' Phoebe fetched *Grimms' Fairy Tales* from the shelf.

'I like it scary.' Tara snuggled down, listening, wide-eyed, to the traditional bloodthirsty version of the story, and giving a sigh of contentment when the evil queen met her doom at the end.

'Phoebe,' she said, when it was over, 'are all stepmothers wicked?'

'I hope not,' Phoebe said ruefully. 'There's a lot of them about these days.'

'Do you think I'll have one?'

Phoebe bit her lip. 'That's your father's business not mine, poppet.'

'Do you think Daddy might marry Mummy again?' It was a forlorn little voice.

'Is that what you want?' Phoebe asked gently.

'Sometimes.'

'The trouble is that people change,' Phoebe said, struggling to find the right words. 'And they don't always want the same things any more.'

'Like Mummy didn't want Daddy and me.'

Phoebe groaned inwardly. 'I'm sure that wasn't how she felt,' she said softly. 'I expect it was very hard for her.'

'She's going to come and see me,' Tara said with drowsy satisfaction. 'She promised the last time she phoned. Then you'll meet her.'

Phoebe forced a smile. 'That will be nice.'

'But it's a secret,' the child warned. 'We mustn't tell anyone, or it won't happen.'

'More secrets?' Dominic asked quizzically as he strolled in.

'The biggest one of all,' Tara assured him, throwing her arms round his neck.

More an unpleasant shock, Phoebe thought ruefully. But it won't happen. She's just stringing the child along.

'Are you going to stay and talk to me?' Tara was asking eagerly.

'No, because it's time you were asleep. I just came to kiss you goodnight.'

'And Phoebe,' said Tara. 'Are you going to kiss her goodnight too?'

There was a silence. Phoebe heard herself swallow, felt a swift flood of warm colour invade her face. Across the bed, she was aware of Dominic watching her, the grey eyes oddly intense.

For one crazy, forbidden moment she let herself wonder how his mouth would feel on hers. She took a step backwards, as if he'd actually reached for her.

And saw his mouth twist as he looked down at his daughter.

'No,' he said. 'I'm not.'

'Why not?'

'Because it isn't her bedtime. At least, not yet,' he added softly. His slow, crooked smile touched Phoebe, sending a long, troublous shiver rippling through her body. She wanted to run—to hide somewhere—but she felt rooted to the spot.

Then he bent and kissed Tara, stroking her cheek gently with a finger as he straightened. 'Sleep well, sweetheart.'

At the door, he turned. 'I'll see you at dinner, Miss Grant,' he said with cool formality.

After he'd gone, there was another silence.

Then, 'I expect he'll kiss you goodnight after dinner,' said Tara. 'Don't you?'

'Tara,' Phoebe said severely, trying to snatch at her composure. 'You're impossible.'

Which, of course, was no real answer at all.

CHAPTER EIGHT

PHOEBE was strongly tempted not to go down to dinner at all.

Changed into her new checked skirt and pink blouse, she sat, staring at herself in the dressing table mirror, wondering what valid excuse she could give to avoid Dominic's company.

But she could think of nothing that he wouldn't see through immediately. Besides which, any open attempt to evade him would betray her own inner turmoil, and that, she thought dispiritedly, would never do.

All she could do was play it cool, and stick rigidly to the limits she'd laid down earlier.

What Dominic might do was another matter altogether.

She left it until the last minute to go downstairs.

In the drawing room, the heavy gold brocade curtains had been drawn against the night. The room was lit by shaded lamps, and by the logs which blazed welcomingly on the hearth.

Dominic was occupying a sofa on one side of the fire. There was a whisky and soda on the table beside him, and he was glancing through the local paper.

He turned as Phoebe entered, his brows lifting as he studied her.

'Carrie's choice, again? I endorse her taste.'

'She's been very kind.' Phoebe, tense as a bow-string, perched on the edge of the opposite sofa.

'Tell me something.' His eyes surveyed her hair, smoothed severely back from her face and confined at

105

the nape of her neck with a barrette. 'Do you never let your hair down, even out of working hours?'

Phoebe reached up a self-conscious hand. 'It's tidier this way,' she said defensively. 'And when you're looking after a child working hours are unpredictable, anyway.'

'Well, you're definitely off-duty this evening.' He paused. 'Would you like a sherry?'

'Oh, no—no thanks.'

'Another tonic water, then?' His mouth twisted a little.

'Nothing—thank you.'

'Have you always been a teetotaller?'

Phoebe looked down at her hands, clasped tightly in her lap. 'I—I learned a long time ago that alcohol doesn't suit me.'

'Pity,' Dominic murmured. 'Because a drink might relax you. You're quite safe, you know,' he added sardonically. 'I never pounce on an empty stomach. Yours, or mine.'

After a startled moment, Phoebe's lips stretched into a reluctant grin.

'That's—very reassuring.' She tried to speak casually.

He said with a touch of crispness, 'Then try and appear reassured.' He paused. 'I have something for you.' He held out a brown envelope.

'A wage packet?' She was bewildered. 'But I've only just started.'

'It's from Mrs Preston at the café. I called in there after we parted company this afternoon, and she asked me to pass it on to you.' He began to tick off on his fingers. 'Your money up to yesterday, plus a week in lieu of notice, and some holiday money.'

Phoebe frowned. 'She doesn't owe me all that.'

He shrugged. 'She certainly thinks so. Argue with her, not me.'

He tossed the envelope towards her, and Phoebe caught it and put it in her skirt pocket.

She said, 'Now I'll be able to repay you for the clothes Carrie bought.'

'There's no hurry for that,' he dismissed. 'Why not indulge yourself with a small shopping spree? I could take you to Midburton tomorrow, after we've dropped Tara at school.'

For a moment, she hesitated. It was ages since she'd had time even for window-shopping. The thought of being able to browse, with money in her pocket, was genuinely tempting.

But she shook her head. 'I'd rather stick to my original intention—if you don't mind.'

'I think I do mind,' he said grimly. 'You really can't bear to be beholden to me—even for a short time—can you?'

There was an almost raw note in his voice. Phoebe bit her lip.

'It isn't that. It has nothing to do with you, only with me,' she said steadily. 'You see, I have this—horror of debt since my father...'

He groaned, shaking his head. 'God, Phoebe, I'm sorry. We seem to be having a competition in paranoia,' he added bitterly.

'I'm not paranoid.'

'Is that a fact? So, you won't mind this?' He walked across the room, took her startled hand and pulled her to her feet, so that she was facing him, her body only inches from his.

'What are you doing?' She tugged herself free, angrily aware she sounded breathless.

'Simply letting you know that dinner is served,' he retorted. 'And I'm hungry even if you're not.'

Phoebe drew a deep breath, and walked ahead of him to the dining room.

They had leek and potato soup, followed by a rich game pie, with *crème brûlée* as dessert. Carrie was a truly wondrous cook, thought Phoebe, doing full justice to the meal in spite of her emotional turmoil.

To her relief, Dominic kept the conversation light, and reasonably impersonal. Perhaps he'd taken her strictures to heart, after all.

'We'll have coffee in the drawing room,' Dominic said as he rose from his chair at the end of the meal.

'I think I'll take mine to the other sitting room,' Phoebe said quickly, watching him pour the brew from a silver pot on a side table. She didn't want to spend any more time than was necessary alone with him here in the warm, lamplit intimacy of the drawing room. 'There—there's something I want to watch on television.'

'Really?' Dominic drawled. 'I didn't have you down as an avid viewer. There was no television at the cottage.'

Phoebe gave him a set smile. 'Not much gets past you, Mr Ashton. But that was the landlord's choice, not mine, I assure you. I love game shows,' she invented wildly. 'Situation comedies—soap operas. In fact, anything that doesn't make me think too hard.' And anything that's going to deter you from joining me, she added silently.

'Then tonight's your night.' Dominic's eyes glinted at her. 'According to the paper, there's international football on one channel and a boxing match on another. Nothing to tax the brain there.'

'No, indeed,' Phoebe agreed woodenly, trying not to grind her teeth. 'Perhaps I'll just have an early night instead.'

'Another excellent idea. In fact I might join you.' As her startled eyes flew to his face, he gave her a mocking grin. 'Not literally, of course. Or were you thinking I might be about to follow up Tara's earlier and quite fascinating suggestion?'

'No, I wasn't,' Phoebe said stonily, furiously aware that she was blushing again.

'Oh, be honest,' he said derisively. 'You've been like a cat on hot bricks all evening, wondering if and when I was going to make my move.'

'That is not true...'

'Then it should have been. Even with your hair scraped back to oblivion, and that just-scrubbed look, you're a vibrant and attractive girl.' He sounded strangely angry. 'You should expect every man you meet to want to kiss you—to make love to you.'

'You mean I should behave like a tart?' She was trembling in every limb, remembering with bitter clarity all the harsh words he'd once thrown at her.

'Of course not,' he said impatiently. 'What the hell are you talking about?'

'This may come as a shock to you, *Mr Ashton*.' She emphasised the formal use of his name. 'But I'm not turned on by this kind of conversation.' She threw her head back. 'Tara's comment was—an embarrassment, and I've taken her to task over it. I didn't expect you to refer to it again,' she added stiffly.

'Oh, really?' His drawl was sceptical. 'Well, it didn't embarrass me. And, as you've brought the subject up, I'd like to know what *would* turn you on, my prim Miss Grant?'

'Nothing,' she said between her teeth. 'Nothing that you could do.'

'You mean you're truly above all those nasty, primitive urges of the flesh?' He shook his head, slowly. 'My God, Phoebe, you must be superhuman.'

'I find this distasteful,' she said curtly. 'There are rules about the employer/hired help relationship, and this— this amounts to sexual harassment.' She walked to the door. 'And I won't bother with coffee. I'm going to my room, and I'd like you to remember what I've said. That's if you want me to stay.'

'And there are a few things that you should remember too, darling.' The anger was out in the open now, and mixed with something else less identifiable. 'This is my house, and I make the rules. Nor am I open to any kind of politically correct blackmail. But as you've made the accusation I may as well commit the crime.'

She snatched at the door handle, trying to turn it, but her fingers slipped. Then Dominic was gripping her shoulders, spinning her to face him, trapping her between the panels of the door and his body. His eyes glittered and the cold purpose in his face made her shrink.

'No,' she whispered. 'Please. You can't...'

'Ah,' he said softly. 'But I can.'

He put his hands on the door, one on either side of her head, holding her imprisoned without touching her. She could feel the warmth of his skin penetrating the layers of her clothing. She could breathe the scent of him, heated, aroused. Could almost hear the uneven race of his heart. Or perhaps it was the pulsation of her own blood, driven by an excitement she'd never experienced before.

She didn't know any more. Her pupils dilated as she stared up into the dark face. Her lips parted in a little sigh, half protest, half capitulation, as his mouth descended slowly to possess hers.

The anger in him had been reined back, brought under control. His lips were gentle but very deliberate, at first just brushing the yielding contours of hers, tantalising them.

One hand stroked her hair, then slid to the nape of her neck, and she felt the barrette give way. Heard it fall to the carpet as the soft strands were released to fall around her face. Heard, too, his soft sigh of satisfaction.

His fingers twisted in her hair, as if it were a silken rope and he, suddenly, her prisoner. And at the same time his kiss deepened, his mouth exploring hers with almost exquisite precision, the tip of his tongue tasting the moist fullness within, every delicate movement creating a new greed, a new yearning.

Her own hands lifted slowly to clasp behind his head and hold him to her. Her mouth offered a first, trembling response to the unhurried pressure of his. Which changed everything.

Dominic pulled her fiercely into his arms, holding her against the urgent thrust of his body. He kissed her hungrily, with a passionate demand that was almost raw in its intensity. With an explicit sensuality which made no concessions to her inexperience.

Concessions that were suddenly no longer necessary, she realised in some dazed, reeling corner of her mind. She wanted to learn everything that he could teach her. To take all that he was offering. To know, and be known in turn.

She was starving, thirsting for him, her mouth ardent, eager, seeking. She was burning up with fever. She was shivering with something that went far beyond mere cold.

Mouths, hands and loins, they clung to each other.

Some lifetime later, he lifted his head. His eyes were slumbrous, and there was a hectic flush painted along his high cheekbones.

He said, in a whisper, 'Now tell me to stop.'

Phoebe slumped back against the door, her head falling forward like a flower with a broken stem as she fought for breath.

She was conscious of him walking away from her. Heard the unsteady chink of the decanter against a glass.

Slowly, she straightened, and looked across the room at him, raising a hand to her bright and swollen mouth.

He said quietly, 'So you're human after all, Miss Grant. Just flesh and blood like the rest of us.' He raised his glass to her in a jeering parody of a toast. 'Now run away to bed,' he went on savagely, 'before I compound my iniquities and take you right here on the floor.'

He paused. 'Or is that what you're waiting for?'

Somehow she was able to move her head in negation.

This time the door handle obeyed her clutching fingers. She slid round the edge of the door like a shadow, and made for the stairs. Halfway up, she tripped and sank to her knees, blinded by tears. Then she dragged herself up, and went on. Closed the door of her bedroom. Turned the key.

And then she looked at herself in the mirror. Saw the blurred reflection of a stranger, with half the buttons on her blouse undone. A mark on her neck where his teeth had grazed.

She thought, What have I done? Oh, dear God, what have I done? And felt a sob shake her whole body.

It was a long time before she could think coherently enough to make a plan.

She would have to leave, of course. After what had just happened, how could she bear to go on living under the same roof with him?

An experiment, she thought, washing away the tearstains. That was all it had been to him. Proof that, for all her brave words, he could make her do anything he wanted.

Even now, her whole body ached and throbbed with arousal.

And she'd allowed him to gain that power over her, she derided herself. She'd left him in no doubt that she wanted him. That he could have had her surrender, if he'd wished.

But, once again, he'd turned away from her. Not in disgust, but in indifference. And somehow the pain of that was more than she could bear, completely transcending the shame of their first encounter six years ago.

Was it for this that she'd slowly rebuilt her self-esteem—just so that he could knock it down again? And all to prove a point.

Oh, you fool, she thought wearily. You pathetic, *criminal* fool.

As she listlessly unzipped her skirt and stepped out of it she heard something crackle in one of the pockets. Mrs Preston's wage packet, she thought, staring at it. And her lifeline out of this house.

Because there was still the call box in the village, and a taxi to safety. Just like last time. Only tonight she would be leaving for ever.

Even better, while she and Dominic had been having dinner Carrie had come up and left her black skirt and white blouse, clean and freshly ironed, on the bed. Her undies were there too.

At least she'd have her own clothes. She would take nothing with her. Nothing he'd paid for.

She would wait until the house was quiet, and then she would go. Carrie had told her there was a spare front door key in the hall-table drawer. She would use that, then post it back through the letter box.

For a moment she visualised Tara's woeful reaction to the news, and Carrie's disappointment, and felt a knife twist inside her.

But I don't have a choice, she placated herself.

She could no longer cope with the ambivalence of her feelings towards Dominic, or the contradictions of life in this house.

She thought, I should never have come back here. I should have dropped Tara at the door and told the driver to take me away.

She dressed, collected her coat, her handbag and her tin box, and lay down on the bed to wait. Dominic's face seemed to swim in front of her, and she closed her eyes to shut him out. She must have dozed off, for when she opened her eyes again the house was dark and silent, and the bedside clock told her it was well after midnight.

Time to go. She put on her coat, picked up her belongings, and let herself out of her room. For a moment she paused, wondering if she should go up to the nursery and say a final, silent goodbye to Tara, and deciding regretfully that it wouldn't be safe.

At the top of the stairs, she cautiously clicked on one of the wall lights in the hall below, and began to make her way down.

She opened the drawer in the table and felt for the key, but it didn't seem to be there. She pulled the drawer further open, wishing she could risk more light.

Then, almost in the next instant, her wish was granted. As light suddenly flooded the hall Phoebe cried out in fright, and turned.

Dominic was standing in the doorway of the drawing room, watching her. He looked haggard, the powerful facial bones stark under his taut skin. There was a smell of whisky, faint but unmistakable.

He said quietly, 'I thought if I waited long enough you'd come.'

'I'm leaving,' she said. 'And you can't stop me.'

'No,' he agreed wearily. 'I probably can't. But there are some things I have to say to you first.'

'I don't want to hear them.' She picked up her tin box from the hall table and hugged it defensively.

'I can understand that too.' He paused. 'I've behaved very badly, Phoebe, and I've no excuse at all.' His mouth twisted wryly. 'Except that you got under my skin from the first moment we met.'

'Is that meant to be an apology?'

'The beginnings of one, perhaps.' The grey eyes never left her. 'I regret what happened earlier more than I can say.'

'Not,' she said, 'as much as I do.'

He winced, but went on. 'You were in my employ, and I had no right to touch you. But you—needled me, and I wanted—' He stopped almost helplessly. 'Hell— to teach you a lesson, I suppose.' His mouth twisted. 'As it was, I think we both learned something.'

Phoebe stiffened. 'Are you trying to say it was my fault?'

'You know exactly what I'm saying. For a while there it was mutual, and you know it. Which,' he continued grimly, 'is all the more reason for it not to happen again.'

'You—you started it,' she accused.

'Yes,' he said. 'And I finished it too. For both our sakes. While I still could. So I'm not completely the black-hearted villain.'

She said raggedly, 'And I'm not some tart—some little slut for you to use as your plaything. I never was...' Her voice tailed off with a little gasp as she realised how close she'd come to a dangerous revelation.

'No,' he said. 'You were entitled to my protection, and my respect, and I let you down on both counts.'

'Well, we agree on something,' she said tightly. 'May I go now?'

'Just give me another minute.' His voice was low—urgent. 'I can't alter what's happened, or wipe it out. But if you leave like this you don't just punish me, you hurt Tara. And she doesn't deserve it. Why should she suffer for my—lack of control?'

'I can't stay here after this.' Her voice sounded hoarse. 'You know I can't.'

'Because you don't trust me to keep my hands off you?' he asked grimly. 'Tonight I lost my head for a while. I've admitted it, and I won't make that mistake again. I can't afford to.'

His mouth tightened. 'I have very different plans for my life. From now on you're my daughter's nanny, and nothing more. And in that role you'll be completely safe here; I swear it.'

Safe from you, perhaps, Phoebe thought bleakly. But what about myself? What about my feelings?

He took a step nearer. 'Phoebe—you came here for

Tara. If we put tonight behind us, couldn't you stay on—for her sake? Just for Tara?'

There was a silence. The pain inside her was subsiding to a dull, hopeless ache. She supposed, in time, she would learn to live with it. That by the time her services were no longer required she might even be inured to this emptiness—this sense of total, bitter loss.

She said hoarsely, 'Very well, then. Just for Tara.'

'Thank you,' he said quietly. 'I promise you won't regret it—not this time.' He paused. 'I'll take Tara to school in the morning and give you a chance to catch up on the sleep you've missed. As long as you collect her in the afternoon.'

She nodded, and turned towards the stairs. Situation normal, and strictly business, she thought. That was how he wanted it. That was how it would be. Just for Tara.

And she knew that while she might fool him she could never deceive herself.

CHAPTER NINE

ROUTINE, thought Phoebe. That's the panacea I need. Establish a pattern to my days, and stick to it.

She'd made a good start. She'd stayed in her room until she heard the Range Rover depart, and then she'd transferred her things up to the nursery suite and installed herself in the room Cindy had used.

And I'll let Carrie know that from now on I'll be taking all my meals with Tara, she told herself resolutely.

Her own sanctuary ready, she started on the nursery itself, tidying Tara's toys into neat rows and sorting out the games and books, stacking them on the shelves provided. In a large wall cupboard she discovered some books with a rather older appeal, many of them with Dominic's name inside, and a pile of jigsaw puzzles. Maybe Tara could tackle one of the simpler ones, with her help.

'My word, you have been busy.' Carrie appeared with an armful of clean linen. 'But I don't approve of you going without breakfast,' she added sternly. 'Even if you did go to bed with a headache last night.' She peered at Phoebe. 'You still look a bit pale.'

'I'm fine,' Phoebe assured her. 'I'll have some toast when I come down for coffee.'

'Everything's ready for you, but you'll have to see to it yourself,' Carrie told her. 'I'm off to Midburton. The Town Stores has just had all its Christmas dried fruit delivered, and I'm planning on making the cake and puddings this weekend.'

'Can I help?'

'You can have a stir—and a wish,' Carrie told her comfortably, and bustled off.

A wish, thought Phoebe as she made Tara's bed. Now that could be dangerous.

Before going on her way downstairs, she stripped off the bed she'd been using and carried the sheets to the laundry room.

Back in the kitchen, she decided against making toast, opting instead for some of Carrie's home-made oatmeal biscuits.

She was sitting at the table, sipping her coffee and glancing at the daily paper, when the door opened and Hazel Sinclair came in, her arms full of bronze chrysanthemums.

She stopped dead when she saw Phoebe.

'You.'

It was difficult to discern whether the word held more shock than annoyance, but on balance, Phoebe thought, annoyance won.

She said politely, 'Good morning, Miss Sinclair. May I offer you some coffee?'

'No, you mayn't. What are you doing here, may I ask?'

'I suppose,' Phoebe returned composedly, 'that I could ask you the same.'

'I should have thought it was perfectly obvious. It occurred to me the other night how bare the place looks. Carrie's housekeeping verges on the basic. It lacks those—gracious touches.'

'To be provided by those chrysanthemums, I suppose?'

'As a matter of fact, yes,' Miss Sinclair snapped. 'Why are you here?'

'I'm acting as Tara's nanny, until Dominic can find a replacement.'

'A nanny? You?' The other woman's voice was derisive. 'That's the last thing I'd have imagined.'

'Well, I didn't have you down as a flower arranger, so we can both be wrong,' Phoebe said, smiling sunnily.

'Are you trying to be insolent?' There were bright spots of colour burning in Miss Sinclair's cheeks.

I'd say I'd succeeded, thought Phoebe.

Aloud, she said neutrally, 'I'm sorry you should think that,' and went back to her paper.

'Well, don't just sit there,' Hazel Sinclair's voice hectored her. 'Find me some vases.'

'I'd be happy to help,' Phoebe replied quietly. 'But I don't know where they are. I'm still not totally familiar with the house.'

'I should think not.' Miss Sinclair snorted. 'Dominic must be out of his mind, taking in some complete stranger off the streets.'

'No,' Phoebe said gently, her blood slowly coming to the boil, 'I was a waitress. At the Clover Tea Rooms, remember?'

'Well, you're still totally unsuitable. I shall have a serious talk with Dominic this evening. That child needs a firm hand—proper discipline. Not some untrained nobody.'

'I totally agree with you,' Phoebe said silkily. 'But Dominic, bless him, seems to think I'm perfect.' She drank the remains of her coffee and stood up. 'Now I'll leave you to your chrysanthemums. Such difficult flowers, I always think,' she added casually. 'But I'm sure you'll bring them to order.'

And she walked out, leaving the other woman staring after her, open-mouthed.

So Hazel Sinclair had the run of the house, she thought unhappily, her bravado deserting her as she went back upstairs. Well, Dominic had dropped a broad enough hint last night about his hopes for the future. And Miss Sinclair's confident behaviour provided total confirmation.

She was shaken by the dislike she felt for the other

woman. And it wasn't simply because Dominic had chosen her to share his life.

She's an arrogant, uncaring bitch, Phoebe thought stormily, and I'd think so whatever circumstances we had met under. Love must really be blind if he can't see it—or if he thinks she'll make a good stepmother for Tara.

She bit her lip. She could see immense problems already looming up on the horizon. But at least she wouldn't be here when they came crashing down.

Although that wasn't the most comforting thought she'd ever had either, she decided morosely.

She stayed upstairs, assuaging the violence of her feelings by scrubbing out the bathroom.

And it was here that Carrie found her on her return.

'My goodness.' She peered around over her glasses. 'You're not employed as a cleaner, you know. I told you that.'

'I needed it.' Phoebe gave her a rueful grin. 'Very cathartic—scrubbing.'

'Hmm.' Carrie pursed her lips and gave Phoebe a shrewd look. 'I saw we'd had a visitor. Never liked chrysanths, myself. Remind me of funerals.' She gave a small, fierce sigh. 'Anyway, lunch is ready. Bacon and egg pie and a winter salad. Come down when you're ready.'

The rest of the day passed peacefully enough. Phoebe drove into Westcombe before picking Tara up from school, and bought herself a new radio to replace the one destroyed in the fire.

She also called in at the tea rooms, to be pounced on by Lynn.

'How's the dishy boss?' She winked at Phoebe. 'He had Mrs P eating out of his hands yesterday. Paying you holiday money wasn't her idea. Mind you,' she added, out of the corner of her mouth, 'I think she'd pay double the amount to get you back. That Debbie's been up to all her old tricks already.'

'Good to know nothing's changed,' Phoebe returned drily, aware of a slight give-away flush at the mention of Dominic.

As she waited at the school gates she was aware of a few measuring glances from the BMW brigade, but a couple of the other nannies smiled and said, 'Hi.'

And Tara, she noticed, frowning, still emerged on her own. But her rather solemn expression vanished when she saw Phoebe.

She came scampering to the car. 'Are you better? Daddy said you had a headache this morning.'

'Oh, that's all gone.' Smiling, Phoebe ruffled her hair.

It's the heartache, she thought with a pang, that's the real trouble.

The evening followed the routine of the previous one, except that Phoebe had supper with Tara, as planned.

'Mr Dominic's dining with friends,' Carrie informed them both.

And I don't have to guess which friends, Phoebe decided with an inward sight.

Tonight there was hotpot with red cabbage, and apple crumble to follow.

'I shall be seriously overweight if this goes on,' Phoebe said, only half joking.

'You could do with more weight,' Carrie advised her crisply. 'Might get rid of that hunted look you've got.'

Once Tara was asleep, Phoebe found herself at something of a loose end. Carrie was busy in the kitchen, weighing out the fruit for her Christmas baking and soaking it in alcohol, and she had made it clear she preferred to manage on her own.

Phoebe wandered into the nursery, took down one of the more complicated jigsaws and emptied the pieces onto the big, battered table. She switched on her new radio, found a channel that was playing music—light and undemanding—and settled down to work.

It was years since she'd done a jigsaw, and she'd forgotten how calming and absorbing they could be.

She'd completed the frame, and done half the sky, when Dominic's voice said grimly behind her, 'So here you are.'

'Well, yes.' She absorbed his frown as he walked round the table and stood opposite her. 'Is there a problem?'

'Hazel tells me you were rude to her this morning.'

'She, of course, was all sweetness and charm.' Phoebe carefully added a leafy twig to a tree.

His mouth tightened. 'That is hardly the point. She was a guest in this house...'

'And I'm the hired help,' Phoebe supplied as he hesitated. 'In future I'll tug my forelock.'

'Oh, for God's sake,' he said impatiently. 'That's not what I meant at all.'

'Then what do you mean?'

He sighed irritably. 'That things are difficult enough, without you creating extra complications.'

Phoebe bit her lip. 'I'm sorry if my misdeeds spoiled your evening.'

'They didn't,' he said curtly.

'But from now on I'll try to be civil.' She added levelly, 'I hope Miss Sinclair will do the same.'

'I'll talk to her—see if I can ease the situation.' He paused. 'Why don't you come downstairs where it's comfortable?'

'Because I'm fine where I am, thanks.' She placed another piece in her puzzle.

'Phoebe.' There was an almost pleading note in his voice. 'I made a solemn promise. You don't have to build a blockade.'

'This is my place,' she said. 'The place I'm making for myself while I'm here. My personal space.' She paused. 'And please start advertising for my replacement soon. I want to be gone by early January.'

'Don't worry,' he tossed back at her. 'I'm in just as much of a hurry as you are.'

Pressure from Hazel Sinclair, no doubt, she thought bitterly, wishing he would go and leave her to her thoughts, however unsatisfactory they might be.

Instead, he picked up the lid of the puzzle box and examined it.

'I remember this one. My godmother gave it to me as a birthday present.' He gave a reminiscent grin. 'I'd been to stay with her in the school holidays and broken a window. I think she wanted to wean me off football and on to some quieter pursuit.'

'I didn't realise it was yours.' Phoebe bit her lip. 'I hope you don't mind—it was just there, in the cupboard.'

'Of course not,' he said. 'But be warned.' He pointed to the sky and the feathery branches of the trees. 'The easy part is over. From now on it gets harder all the time.'

Tell me about it, she thought as he left the room. She could hear him descending the stairs, and realised that she wanted very badly to cry.

'Oh, to hell with it,' she said raggedly, and swept the uncompleted puzzle back into the box. 'Who needs any more complications?'

It was strange, she thought, how quickly everything seemed to fall into place. How life assumed a stable daily pattern, which was, at least, bearable.

While Tara was at school she had a considerable amount of time to herself, and, with the luxury of a car, she set out to explore the district.

The weather had turned cold and crisp, with sunshine most days, and she could smell woodsmoke in the air as she drove.

The end of the year, she thought, and, for her, the finale of a whole phase of her life. And who knew what could be round the corner? She had to keep looking forward, because anything else was too painful.

She saw very little of Dominic, and it was better that way. He left for his offices in Midburton first thing in the morning, and often returned only briefly in the evening to dine, and then go out again. Certainly he'd accepted her absence from his dinner table without comment. Perhaps he was even relieved that she'd taken the initiative.

And certainly he and Hazel Sinclair seemed almost inseparable, although the other woman hadn't made any more lightning descents on the house when he'd been away.

But she could bide her time, Phoebe acknowledged wretchedly. Before too long she'd be living there, mistress of all she surveyed. Free to make any changes she wished, too.

Carrie was discreet, but Phoebe could tell she was worried about the future. And there was little doubt that Tara would be shuffled off to boarding school.

Preparations for Christmas had moved into gear. Tara was diligently practising her rendition of 'Away in a Manger'. She'd added the words now, and the sound of her high, sweet little voice brought a lump to Phoebe's throat.

The cake and puddings were finished, and stored away, and both Tara and Phoebe had stirred the mixtures and dutifully made their wishes.

'I wished for Mummy to come for Christmas,' Tara confided solemnly. 'But I don't expect my wish will come true.'

And nor, thought Phoebe, will mine.

One afternoon, when Phoebe collected Tara from school, it was a tearstained, woebegone figure who climbed into the car.

'Darling, what's the matter?' Phoebe asked in consternation.

'Our class is doing a nativity play for the last day of term,' Tara sobbed. 'Mrs Franks chose people for all the parts this afternoon and I 'ditioned for the Virgin Mary. I had to sing "Away in a Manger", and Mrs Franks said I'd cheated because I knew it too well. So now I haven't got a part at all—and I'm the only one,' she added on a little wail.

'Sit there,' Phoebe ordered grimly. 'I'm going to see about this.'

Mrs Franks's smile was acid when she saw Phoebe. 'Can I help you with something?'

'Yes,' Phoebe said steadily. 'I'd like to know why Tara Ashton, my charge, has been excluded from the class nativity play.'

'It was a disciplinary measure,' Mrs Franks said coldly. 'The audition carol for the leading part had been deliberately kept secret to give every child an equal opportunity, and yet Tara managed a polished performance. It was clear to me that she'd found out somehow, and practised to give herself an unfair advantage. Now she has to learn that underhand methods will get her nowhere.'

'Tara has learned "Away in a Manger",' Phoebe agreed, levelly. 'But at her piano lessons as a Christmas surprise for her father. The fact it was an audition piece too is a complete coincidence.'

'Well, I only have your word for that.' Mrs Franks pursed her lips. 'But it makes no difference. Tara has had an ego problem ever since she came to the school. We hear far too much about her mother's Hollywood career,' she added with distaste. 'Perhaps this will teach her not to put herself forward quite so much.'

'And that,' Phoebe said shakily, 'is one of the cruellest and most heartless statements I've ever heard. Goodbye.'

Not surprisingly, Tara didn't want to go to her music lesson that evening, but begged to go home.

When Phoebe stopped off at Mrs Blake's house to explain, she found the other woman more than understanding.

'Poor little soul,' she said indignantly. 'But I'm not surprised. I've never cared for that school.' She wrinkled her nose. 'It's very much geared to one social set, and they seem more interested in who does what at the Pony Club than academic achievement.' She hesitated. 'And Tara may have an extra black mark against her for being Serena Vane's daughter.'

'You mean you think she does have an ego problem?' Phoebe asked, troubled.

'No, on the contrary.' Celia Blake shook her head. 'But a few years ago Miss Vane used to throw some pretty wild parties when she was down here. Parties to which male guests did not bring their wives,' she added darkly. 'A lot of local husbands blotted their copybooks in a big way, and that hasn't been forgiven, or forgotten. I suspect Tara's problem may not be with her classmates but their mothers.'

'Oh, how ridiculous,' Phoebe said indignantly. 'None of that can possibly be Tara's fault.'

'No, but I suspect she's a victim of prejudice just the same.' Celia sighed. 'It's a pity Mr Ashton didn't opt for the village school at Fitton Magna. I go there to take singing, and though it's only small it has excellent standards, and a really happy atmosphere. And none of the social pressures of Westcombe Park,' she added drily.

'I'll talk to him about it this evening,' Phoebe said with resolution.

Back at the house, she handed Tara over to Carrie, who led her away, clucking, for a hot drink and biscuits. Then, drawing a deep breath, she went to find Dominic.

He was standing beside the desk in his study, reading through some faxes. His briefcase was standing open on the desk beside him and he looked preoccupied, and a little remote. Phoebe hesitated for a moment, then tapped lightly on the open door.

When he saw who it was, he seemed to stiffen momentarily. His smile was brief, and forced.

'Is something the matter?'

'Yes, I'm afraid so.' Phoebe gave him a brief résumé of the day's events at Westcombe Park School. 'Tara's naturally very upset, and I think she has cause.'

'Yes,' he said heavily. 'And you saw this coming, didn't you?' He gave her a wintry smile. 'Unfortunately, there's nothing I can do immediately. I have to go away tonight, and I could be gone for anything up to a week. I was just about to find her to say goodbye.'

Phoebe bit her lip. 'That will be another blow,' she told him quietly. 'She hardly sees you nowadays.'

'Has she complained?' he asked sharply.

'Not in so many words.' Phoebe lifted her chin. 'But then she wouldn't.' She paused. 'You couldn't delay your trip just for one day?'

He shook his head. 'It's out of the question. A company I helped a while back is the subject of a hostile takeover, and I'm trying to create a rescue package for them.'

'And your young daughter?' Her voice was husky. 'What about a rescue package for her?'

The grey eyes met hers with ice in their depths.

'That,' said Dominic, 'is what I pay you for.'

'And that,' Phoebe said shakily, 'is a bloody awful thing for a father to say.'

There was a pregnant silence, then Dominic lifted his hands in surrender.

'All right,' he said wearily. 'I can't do anything about this trip, but I swear when I get back—'

'Don't mention quality time,' she interrupted. 'Or I might hit you.'

She couldn't believe what she'd just said, and, to judge by his face, neither could he.

But the bleakness faded from his face, to be replaced by reluctant amusement. 'You might try,' he told her drily. 'And I was going to say that I shall devote myself to her interests, including sorting out this school business. Is that acceptable?'

'I'm—sorry,' Phoebe stammered. 'It's just that she loves you so much—and you're missing out too.'

'It's good of you to think of me,' he said mockingly. 'Given the violence of your feelings.'

He looked at his watch. 'Hell, I've got to go. Is Tara watching television?' He barely waited for her answering nod before striding out of the room and across the hall.

Phoebe lingered, not wishing to intrude, wanting them to have at least this brief time together.

Then there was a strident peal of the doorbell, and Hazel Sinclair swept in, bringing a wave of cold air mixed with Poison.

'Where's Dominic?' she demanded imperiously. 'He hasn't left yet?'

'Not yet. But he's just saying goodbye to Tara. He may not want to be disturbed.'

Hazel gave Phoebe the kind of look most people reserve for woodlice.

'Don't be absurd,' she said crushingly. 'Are they upstairs?'

'No, they're in the small sitting room,' Phoebe admitted.

'More television, I suppose?' Hazel sniffed. 'I'd have thought you could have thought up something more intellectually stimulating for the child. Especially in view of the salary you're being paid,' she added sharply. 'But you girls are all the same—creating a generation of couch potatoes, just so that you can have an easy life.'

And she walked off, leaving Phoebe to follow, smarting.

'Dominic, darling.' Phoebe heard the honeyed greeting followed by a crisper, 'Good evening, Tara.'

'Hazel.' Dominic's tone was surprised, and held a faint reserve. 'I wasn't expecting you.' He was sitting beside the fire, with a watery-eyed Tara on his knee. He put the little girl down gently, and stood up.

'I know, my sweet, but I had to catch you before you went away.' She paused dramatically. 'I've got the most wonderful news. You remember the Claytons, of course—Howard and Linnet? Well, they've taken a house just outside Innsbruck for the whole of Christmas and the New Year.'

'Good for them.' Dominic frowned. 'But I don't see why you had to dash round here to tell me that.'

Hazel sighed elaborately. 'That's only the beginning. They've invited me out there for the whole of the holiday.' She gave an excited little laugh. 'Christmas in Innsbruck, darling. Wonderful food, marvellous skiing. Won't it be heavenly?'

'Paradise on earth,' he agreed courteously. 'I hope the snow stays deep and crisp and even for you.'

'Not just for me, darling.' She pouted playfully. 'For *us*. They want me to bring my—partner.'

There was an astonished silence, broken by a sudden tearful roar from Tara.

'No,' she screamed, her face contorted. 'You're not taking my daddy away for Christmas. I won't let you. You're an old witch and I hate you.'

'That's enough.' Phoebe and Dominic spoke in unison as Hazel turned crimson.

'Well,' Hazel said with a metallic laugh. 'One can see who's become completely out of hand.' She looked inimically at Phoebe. 'And the reason.'

Tara wilted instantly. She took her father's hand. 'Daddy, you won't go—will you?' she pleaded woefully. 'You won't leave me?'

Dominic crouched down beside her. 'It could be fun,' he said gently. 'You've never learned to ski.'

'Dominic,' Hazel intercepted, 'I'm afraid that's out of the question. It's a grown-up party. Howard and Linnet have no children. They couldn't cope—wouldn't want to...' Her voice tailed away.

He got to his feet. 'Then I wouldn't want to either,' he said calmly.

'You mean you're turning down the invitation? Oh, I don't believe it.' For a moment Hazel sounded hysterical, then she visibly pulled herself together, even managing a smile. 'Clearly we can't talk about it now. You have to go. But think it over carefully while you're away, and we'll discuss it when you return.'

There was a pause, then Dominic said, 'Very well.' He turned to Phoebe. 'Take Tara downstairs, will you? It must be her suppertime.'

'Supper,' Hazel echoed. 'If I'd dared speak to an adult like that at her age, I'd have been sent to bed without any supper.'

Phoebe saw Tara shrink. She said quietly, 'You chose rather a bad moment, Miss Sinclair. But Tara's sorry now, and would like to tell you so.'

There was a silence, then Tara, eyes downcast, muttered an apology.

Dominic dropped a swift kiss on her hair. 'That's better,' he told her. 'Now, be good for Phoebe, and I'll be back before you know it.'

'But I want to wave goodbye,' Tara objected.

Phoebe hastily intervened. 'You can wave from the nursery window.' She hustled the little girl, still protesting, from the room.

'Why do I have to go upstairs?' she demanded.

'Because Daddy wants to say goodbye to Miss

Sinclair now, and we'd be in the way,' said Phoebe, feeling only the truth would serve.

'I wish Miss Sinclair would go away,' Tara said morosely.

So do I, thought Phoebe. But I have an awful feeling that she's here to stay.

Together they watched from the window as Dominic emerged onto the floodlit drive. Hazel was with him, her arm tucked through his, leaning intimately against him. Her face was turned up towards him and she was smiling, talking eagerly, their recent difference apparently forgotten.

At the side of the Range Rover, they paused. Phoebe saw Dominic bend towards her, and Hazel wind her arms round his neck, drawing him down to her for a passionate kiss.

Phoebe turned away, not wanting to see any more.

After a moment Tara joined her, solemn-faced. 'Phoebe—would you mind if I don't have any supper? I don't feel very hungry.' Her lip quivered. 'I don't want Daddy to go away with her.'

Phoebe gave her a quick hug. 'He won't go. He said so. Everything will be fine, you'll see.'

And she wished, with a heavy heart, that she could believe it.

CHAPTER TEN

TARA was flushed and heavy-eyed the next morning, and complained that she didn't feel very well. She produced a convincing cough, so Phoebe allowed her the benefit of the doubt, and rang the school to excuse her.

She didn't feel magnificent herself. She'd spent a restless night with troubled dreams, and had woken with a headache.

A day without pressure might do us both good, she thought.

'What lessons will you be missing?' she asked.

'No lessons.' Tara's lips quivered. 'They're going to be practising the play.'

'Oh, well,' Phoebe said stoutly. 'Then you can practise your surprise for Daddy.'

Tara shook her head. 'I don't want to do that any more. It's all spoiled.'

'You may change your mind later,' Phoebe told her gently, mentally cursing Mrs Franks and all her works.

Tara was silent for a moment. Then she asked, 'Can I sleep in Daddy's room while he's away?'

'I don't know,' Phoebe said, surprised. 'We'll have to ask Carrie.'

'She'll let me,' Tara said confidently.

Which proved to be the case.

'Of course she can, the mite,' Carrie said warmly. 'If it makes her feel closer to him. You can give me a hand to change the linen,' she added briskly.

'Oh.' Phoebe's throat tightened. 'Yes—of course.'

Another hurdle to be surmounted, she thought. Up to that moment she'd never had cause to enter Dominic's

132

bedroom, and on the rare occasions when the door had been open she'd scuttled past, with her face averted.

Like Bluebeard's chamber, she thought, swallowing, it had been the focal point for so many nightmares over the years. Maybe going in there to do a simple, practical task might now lay them to rest for ever. But she couldn't be sure, and she might find herself condemned again to the dark, torturous world of memory.

Her jaw felt taut, and her fists were clenched as she followed Carrie into the room. And stopped, her lips parting in a gasp of astonishment. Because this was not the room she remembered.

The dark red walls were now papered in a creamy shade with a faint gold stripe, and the canopied bed had disappeared entirely, replaced by a wide, modern divan with a heavy bronze silk coverlet. The rest of the furniture was different too.

I wouldn't have known the place, she thought, relief flooding over her.

'Nice, isn't it?' Carrie misread her expression. 'Mr Dominic had it all redone when his marriage ended. And small blame to him. No one would want to sleep with his kind of memories.'

Or mine, thought Phoebe.

'When are we going to get the Christmas tree?' Tara asked eagerly over lunch. 'We could decorate it to welcome Daddy back.'

'That's a nice idea.' Phoebe smiled at her, glad to see that she was looking far less woebegone.

'Mr Dominic's got an account at Harvey's Nurseries,' Carrie put in. 'Choose the one you want, and they'll deliver it.'

'Can we go this afternoon?' Tara begged. 'Only I have to be home by teatime, because Daddy's promised to phone me every evening.'

Phoebe's heart skipped a painful beat. 'Then we'd better hurry,' she returned lightly.

The big shed at the nurseries where the trees were stored smelt deliciously of pine. There were a number of other people engaged on the same leisurely task. The real rush had still to begin.

After a lot of debate, Phoebe and Tara settled for a medium-sized tree which still had its own roots.

'Then we can plant it in the garden after Christmas,' Tara said happily.

The rest of the afternoon was occupied by sorting through the big box of baubles and tree hangings that Carrie had unearthed from a cupboard, and constructing from thin wire, cardboard and some old lace curtains an angel to occupy the top of the tree. She wore rather too much lipstick for a real seraph, and her halo was appropriately lop-sided, but Tara thought she was perfect.

She had a lot to tell Dominic during the precious phone call. Phoebe could hear her racing excitedly on out in the hall.

Dominic, she thought, would be lucky to get a word in. But apparently he managed it, because suddenly Tara came flying in.

'Daddy wants a word,' she announced. She looked suddenly apprehensive. 'I hope he isn't cross because I didn't go to school.'

So do I, thought Phoebe wryly.

But the deep voice was alive with amusement. 'Is this the same woeful scrap we had to comfort yesterday?'

'It seems so.' Phoebe hesitated. 'Did she mention that she's moved into your room? I—I hope you don't mind.'

'As long as she doesn't imagine it's a long-term arrangement,' he returned drily. 'I have other plans.'

Phoebe bit her lip. 'Yes—of course.'

'Are you all right?' His voice was suddenly sharp. Even miles away, he didn't miss a nuance.

'Fine,' she said ultra-brightly. 'I've had a splendid day.'

'Mine hasn't been too bad either.' He paused. 'I may be back sooner than I expected.'

She despised herself for the swift lift of her heart that his words induced.

She said sedately, 'That's good.'

'I hope so,' he said gravely. 'After all, we have a lot to talk about.'

She said hurriedly, 'I think Tara's education should be a priority.'

She heard something that might have been a sigh. 'Yes, I'm sure you do. But we'll discuss the agenda when I get there.' He paused again. 'Goodnight, Phoebe. Be good. Keep safe.'

She replaced the receiver slowly, aware of the flutter of her pulses. His parting words seemed to enfold her like strong arms.

Only it was far too late for safety now, she acknowledged, sighing in her own turn as she returned to the drawing room.

'You're all pink,' said Tara, adding reflectively, 'I think we should buy some mistletoe.'

Phoebe thought she might have trouble getting Tara to bed that night, but the little girl behaved with total docility, sliding under the covers of the vast bed with her favourite teddy.

'The sooner I go to sleep, the sooner it will be another day and Daddy will come back,' she confided.

'I can't argue with that.' Phoebe kissed her goodnight.

Carrie had gone to the village Women's Institute Christmas party, and the house seemed deathly quiet and empty.

Phoebe tidied away the unused decorations, decided it would be best to shop for some fresh tinsel, and fetched the step-stool for a last attempt at straightening the angel's halo.

'That's better,' she said rather breathlessly, after a brief struggle.

'Much,' an amused male voice commented from behind her, and hands closed on her waist, lifting her down from the stool.

Even as her lips parted in a yelp of fright she knew that she recognised the voice. She wrenched herself free, spinning round, her heart in her mouth.

'Tony—Tony Cathery,' she said unsteadily. 'What the hell are you doing here?'

'I could ask you the same thing,' he said, looking equally taken aback. 'Where's old Dom?'

'He's not here at the moment.' Phoebe gave him a look of loathing. 'Don't tell me he's expecting you?'

He laughed. 'I wouldn't go that far, but he knows I keep turning up, like a bad penny.' His own glance was appraising. 'What's your excuse?'

'I work here,' she said huskily. 'I'm his daughter's nanny.'

'Seriously?' His brows lifted. 'Well,' he said, 'there's a turn-up for the books. So your original brief encounter has all been forgiven and forgotten?'

Phoebe hesitated fatally. 'Naturally.'

'Fascinating,' he said softly. 'Now, I got the opposite impression from Dom. But they do say that time is a great healer.' He crossed to the drinks table and poured himself a generous whisky.

'Care to join me?' He waved the decanter at her. 'Oh, no, I was forgetting. You prefer vodka.'

'You disgust me,' Phoebe said slowly.

Tony laughed. 'That isn't how you used to feel, my sweet. There was a time when you couldn't get enough of me.'

Phoebe walked to the door. 'I think you'd better leave.'

'Ordering me out? That's a bit rich coming from a nanny, darling, to a member of the family.' He smiled maliciously at her startled expression. 'You didn't know that Dom and I were tenuously related, did you? Which proves that you and he have never discussed the events of six years ago. Because he'd have told you, for sure.'

'My God.' Phoebe remembered an earlier conversation with Carrie. 'You're his stepbrother.'

'Got it in one,' he said negligently. He drank some of the whisky, watching her reflectively. 'So, it's still a big secret. How interesting—and how useful.'

Phoebe lifted her chin. 'Why so?'

'Well, for one thing you can stop giving me orders,' he said with sudden coldness. 'That is, if you want your pitiful attempt at seduction to remain a secret. And I don't think you'd last long if Dom knew who you really were.' He tutted. 'Just imagine him letting the little slag he threw out of his house look after his precious child.'

He shook his head sadly. 'He said some pretty rotten things to me too—almost unforgivable actually. And I was only trying to organise his usual welcome. Serena, you see, used to greet him like that—when she was in the mood. Problem was, she used to greet a lot of people in the same way, including myself. And Dom caught us together. In his room. On his bed.'

He grimaced. 'Big mistake. I became seriously *persona non grata*, and so did poor Serena. So I tried to get back into his good books by providing him with compensation. After all, one naked blonde on a bed is pretty much like another. Except that you were totally inexperienced,' he added. 'And Dom might have enjoyed the contrast after Serena's—accomplishments.'

He looked her over. His smile made Phoebe feel dirty. 'I might have enjoyed you myself, actually. You improved one hundred per cent once we'd got your kit off. An amazing little body.'

Phoebe took a deep breath. 'I don't know what you're

trying to achieve, but it's not working. I'd like you to go.'

'Well, there we differ.' Tony poured himself some more whisky. 'Because I'm staying. I suppose Dom's still got that old dragon of a housekeeper? Roust her out, will you, and get her to knock me up a meal.'

'She's out,' Phoebe said shortly.

His smile widened. 'And I suspect anything you cooked for me might not do me any good.' He shrugged. 'I'll have to go to the pub. Would you like to come with me?'

'No,' she said. 'I wouldn't.'

'Of course,' he said. 'You have to babysit.'

'Yes,' she said. 'But that makes no actual difference. Even if I were free, I wouldn't come with you.'

He sighed theatrically. 'Well, that's me told. And yet once you'd have walked over broken glass to get to me. How fickle you are.'

'No,' she said. 'I just grew up, that's all.'

He was still smiling, but there was no amusement in the blue eyes. 'Then I shall eat alone.'

'They do rooms as well,' she threw after his retreating figure.

But it was sheer bravado, she acknowledged once she was alone. Inwardly she was shaking like a leaf, unable to credit what had just happened.

It was like some macabre joke, she thought numbly.

She found she was wandering round the room, walking from the fireplace to the window, over to the tree to make some minor adjustment, and back again.

Calm down, she adjured herself, swallowing. Or you're letting him win. He can't hurt you any more...

Only that wasn't strictly true, she reminded herself wretchedly. He could do a lot of damage, if he wanted.

Dominic clearly had no illusions about him, but he trusted her, and she wanted it to stay that way. She couldn't face his contempt. Not again. Because this time it would destroy her for ever.

She sat down and picked up the paper, but the words swam before her eyes in a meaningless blur.

When the phone rang suddenly, she nearly jumped out of her skin. She went out into the hall and picked up the receiver with trembling hands.

'Hello?' she said uncertainly.

'Phoebe?'

She gasped. 'Oh, Dominic, it's you. Is—is something wrong?'

'I was just about to ask you the same thing,' he returned.

She bit her lip. 'No—everything's fine,' she returned constrainedly. 'I was just surprised to hear from you again.'

'I wanted to talk to you when Tara was out of the way.' He paused. 'That is allowed under the agreement, I hope? You don't feel you have to fetch Carrie as chaperon?'

In spite of herself, she laughed. 'I think we can trust ourselves.'

'I was going to mention this last night, but other events intervened. There's a craft shop in Midburton with an amazing dolls' house for sale. I wondered about buying it as Tara's Christmas present. What do you think?'

'It sounds really good. Has it got furniture?'

'No, they make that separately. I want you to go over there and have a look, and reserve it if you approve. Pick out some furniture too, and tell them to send an invoice to my office. They're expecting you, so they won't sell it over our heads.'

'Oh, I'd love that.' Phoebe remembered her own dolls' house, and the hours of pleasure and happy daydreams it had brought her. 'That makes up for—' She stopped abruptly, aware she was on dangerous ground.

'Makes up for what?' He sounded concerned.

'Oh—general dreariness,' she invented hastily. 'You know.'

'What happened to the splendid day?'

'It—ended.'

'So did mine. It's pretty depressing here too.' He paused. 'I wish I was at home.'

'So do I,' she admitted unguardedly.

'Why, Phoebe.' There was laughter in his voice, but no mockery. 'Can I take it you're missing me?'

'I was thinking of Tara,' she said primly.

A slight sound made her turn her head. To her horror, she saw Tony standing in the doorway which led to the kitchen quarters.

'I—I'd better go,' she told Dominic.

'Condemning me to my hotel room and cable television? That isn't very kind.' His voice sounded odd, almost wistful—but the telephone distorted everything.

'I'm sure there are lots of things you could do.' Phoebe was burningly aware of the eavesdropper a few yards away. 'I've loads of jobs myself.'

'Then I'm sorry I disturbed you.' He was courteous, but there was no more laughter. 'Please don't forget about the dolls' house.'

'I'll see to it first thing tomorrow, after I've taken Tara to school.' She was about to add, Maybe I can get some tiny dolls and dress them for her, when she realised he'd rung off.

Slowly she replaced her own receiver.

'Your esteemed employer, I presume, ringing for a little bedtime chat? How cosy. Is this a regular occurrence?'

Phoebe bit her lip. 'I thought you'd gone to the pub.'

'No, I decided to make myself a sandwich instead. I didn't want to come back and find I'd been locked out,' Tony returned silkily. 'Is Carrie back yet? I need a bed making up.'

'No, she isn't,' Phoebe told him shortly.

He tutted. 'Then you'll have to do it yourself, nanny dear. Unless you'd like me to share your bed?' he added, eyeing her speculatively.

'No, I wouldn't,' Phoebe said calmly. 'And what makes you think Dominic will allow you to stay under his roof?'

'It is Christmas—the time of goodwill. Or do you think I'm stretching brotherly love too far?'

'Yes, I do.'

'Then it's a good job he isn't here.' He made an impatient gesture. 'Look, Phoebe, I need somewhere to sleep for a couple of nights. Help me out on this, and I won't tell Dom your dark secret. Is it a deal?'

'I suppose I can't really stop you,' she said tautly. 'But you can make up your own bed.'

He winced. 'The years haven't improved you, Phoebe. You never used to be this hard. Where are you sleeping?'

'That's none of your business.'

He shrugged. 'Please yourself—but don't blame me if I lose my way, and come blundering in during the night.'

'All right,' she said curtly. 'I'm sleeping in Dominic's room.'

His brows rose. 'Really, darling? How Freudian. Or is this the usual arrangement? In spite of everything, have two lonely hearts begun to beat as one?' He whistled. 'It would explain the intimate phone call.'

'It's to keep Tara company,' she said flatly. 'And she'll already be asleep, so keep out.'

Tony shrugged again. 'Fine. But you don't know what you're missing.'

Phoebe flayed him with a look. 'On the contrary,' she said. 'I know exactly.'

She went out of the room and up the stairs. She collected a few necessities from her own room, then went softly down to Dominic's and tiptoed in.

Tara was indeed fast asleep, and did not stir when Phoebe gingerly lifted the covers and crept in beside her.

She felt deathly tired, but sleep was elusive. As soon as she tried to relax, her mind went into pandemonium over the evening's revelations.

All those years, she thought. All those years I hated Dominic. Blamed him for cruelty and insensitivity when all the time he must have been totally traumatised himself.

What must he have felt—finding his wife with his own stepbrother? she wondered helplessly. And then, after all that, to find himself the victim of a sadistic practical joke.

Tony had used and betrayed them both, she thought, but Dominic's suffering had to be greater than her own. His scarring deeper, and more bitter. The treachery he'd endured was unforgivable.

And all I saw was the anger and contempt, she thought wretchedly. I never noticed his pain—his humiliation. Never stopped to ask why he'd overreacted so violently. I only thought of myself.

Not that it would have made any real difference, she acknowledged, sighing. She and Dominic had been fated to meet at totally the wrong moment in their lives.

And now there would never be a right one. Because Dominic's course in life was set, and Hazel Sinclair would be sharing it with him, for good or ill.

She turned onto her side and wept for the hurt of it all, the waste and the sorrow.

But she wept silently, so as not to disturb Dominic's sleeping child.

Because, ultimately, caring for Tara was all she had. The one gift of love that she dared offer him. And the only one that he would accept from her.

When really she wanted to give him her heart and soul.

CHAPTER ELEVEN

'WHAT'S Uncle Tony doing here?' Tara asked over breakfast the following morning.

'That's what we'd all like to know,' Carrie muttered as she filled the toast rack.

'I'm sorry,' Phoebe said, not for the first time. 'I didn't know what to do. He just—walked in, you see.'

'He'd have walked out again if I'd been here,' Carrie said grimly. 'And what Mr Dominic will say, I've no idea.'

'Doesn't Daddy like Uncle Tony?' Tara was round-eyed. 'Mummy likes him. He came to see us in London.'

Phoebe pretended not to see the speaking glance Carrie was directing at her.

'Uncle Tony's just passing through,' she said briskly. 'And I think it might be better to let him do just that, and not bother Daddy about him. Especially if they don't get on very well.'

Tara considered that, her head on one side. Then she asked, 'Why did you sleep with me last night, Phoebe?'

'It's a very big bed. I was afraid you might get lost.' Phoebe smiled at her. 'Did you mind?'

'No, it was like having a sister.' Tara sighed as she spread honey messily on her toast. 'I've always wanted a sister.'

'Two like you in the house? More than flesh and blood could stand,' Carrie said gruffly, and Tara, not fooled in the least, gave her a serene smile.

Perhaps the prospect of siblings would help reconcile Tara to her father's marriage to Hazel Sinclair, Phoebe told herself as she collected the little girl's things ready for school. That was if Hazel wanted children. She certainly had no interest in Tara. Quite the contrary, in fact. But maybe she'd be different with her own.

As she came down to the hall Tony came out of the drawing room, and stood smiling up at her.

'So there you are.'

'Top marks for observation,' Phoebe said shortly, trying to edge round him, but he was deliberately blocking her path to the door.

'Taking Tara to school? I'll come with you.'

'There's no need for that.'

'Probably not, but I'm coming anyway. I'd like to spend part of the day with someone who's pleased to see me,' he added with something of an edge.

'Under the circumstances, you can hardly expect the red carpet.' Phoebe contributed some edge of her own.

As she unlocked the car, Tara came racing out.

'Uncle Tony, are we going out for a treat?'

'Nothing I'd like more, angel.' He lifted her and swung her round. 'But Nanny says you have to go to school.'

'Oh.' Tara directed a pleading look at Phoebe. 'Do I have to?'

'Absolutely.' Phoebe found herself stiffening with distaste at the sight of Tara in Tony's arms. She met his eyes over the child's head, and realised he knew exactly how she felt and relished it.

'Tell you what, sweetpea, why don't I take you to school this morning in my car?'

'No,' Phoebe said swiftly, and forcefully.

'Lighten up, Feeb.' He was laughing at her openly now. 'Don't be a spoilsport all your life.' Still carrying Tara, he strode towards the raffish sports car parked on the drive.

'Sorry it's only a two seater,' he called back over his shoulder. 'See you later.'

* * *

'It's not your fault.' Carrie poured Phoebe a consolatory cup of coffee. 'He was always the same—selfish, headstrong, and hell-bent on getting his own way. He'll seem glamorous to the child at first, but the novelty will soon wear off for him, mark my words.'

'I should have stopped him somehow,' Phoebe said wretchedly. 'I don't want him playing games with her emotions.' She saw Carrie's surprised look, and added defensively, 'I don't think he's a suitable companion for a child.'

Carrie patted her hand. 'Try not to worry,' she advised. 'He'll be off before you know it, and we can have some peace again.'

As soon as Carrie had gone upstairs to change the towels, Phoebe rang Westcombe Park School. To her surprise and relief, she learned that Tara had been deposited at the school and was now in her classroom, instead of heaven knew where on some jaunt.

And Tony himself returned some ten minutes later.

'Coffee,' he remarked. 'How civilised. I notice Dom's dragon didn't offer me any breakfast this morning.'

'Just what the hell are you playing at?' Phoebe blazed at him. 'Tara is in my care, and you had no right to go against me like that.'

'Afraid I'd kidnapped her?' He gave her a malicious grin. 'No chance. She's a charmer, of course, like any daughter of Serena's would be, but a little of any child's company goes a long way with me.'

'I'd like you to leave her alone.'

'No sooner said than done.' He poured himself some coffee and came to sit opposite her. 'I shall be moving on presently.'

'Moving on?' Phoebe repeated in bewilderment.

'You sound disappointed, honey pie. But in spite of the flawless hospitality I have to tear myself away.'

She eyed him warily. 'That isn't the impression you gave last night.'

'Well,' Tony said lightly, 'perhaps I've had time to think since then. Time to realise that my presence here really wouldn't be welcomed by my dear stepbrother. You see, I have some tact.'

'Why did you come here in the first place?'

He waved an airy hand. 'Family business, darling. But it can wait.' He drank some coffee. 'It's been fascinating to meet you again, in spite of this distressing waspishness you've developed. And do remember that my visit is our little secret.'

'What about Tara and Carrie?' she countered. 'Are they supposed to keep quiet about it too?'

'Oh, Tara's no problem. We have an agreement, she and I. And Carrie's always hated me. She can be easily persuaded to forget I was ever here.'

'It's all perfectly simple, really,' Phoebe said with heavy irony.

'So let's keep it that way.' He finished his coffee and pushed his chair back. He smiled at her, his eyes lingering on her breasts. 'Goodbye, honey pie. Enjoy your nights in Dom's bed. Something tells me there won't be many of them.'

Phoebe was still sitting, staring into space, when Carrie returned ten minutes later.

'I thought I heard a car. Has he gone?'

'Yes,' Phoebe agreed frowningly. 'He has.'

'So that's all right, then,' Carrie said comfortably.

Is it? thought Phoebe, troubled. I wish I could be so sure.

She tried to put Tony's mysterious appearance, and equally enigmatic departure, out of her mind for the trip to Midburton.

The craft shop was at the end of a small precinct, which it shared with a perfumery, a silversmith and a boutique selling hand-painted silk scarves.

The dolls' house was even better than Phoebe had

hoped, spacious and solidly built in a traditional design, with gables and mullioned windows. The whole of the front was on hinges, and the main door and windows all opened.

'It's beautiful,' she told the woman who ran the shop. 'I'd love it myself.'

The other woman laughed. 'I'm glad it's going to a good home. We were all so glad when Mr Ashton came back to Midburton.' She lowered her voice. 'Such a shame about his marriage breaking up. She used to buy her scent in the shop next door, and she was the most lovely thing I ever saw. So charming and natural. Such a *giving* person.'

'So I gather,' Phoebe agreed without expression. 'May I look at the furniture now?'

'It's all hand-made.' The woman passed her a card. 'This is the name of the craftsman if you want to place any special orders. Some people like those big four-poster beds, but we don't keep them in stock.'

'I don't think so.' Phoebe forced a smile. She lingered over her selection, concentrating on basics because Tara would obviously want to choose some things for herself at a later stage.

'If you want to leave the house and furniture until Christmas Eve that will be fine,' the woman offered as she totted up the bill. 'It's often a problem to hide something as big as this.'

'Thanks,' Phoebe accepted gratefully. 'But I'll take some of these little jointed dolls with me now.'

'This is one very lucky little girl.' The woman was wreathed in smiles as she showed Phoebe to the door.

Not in every way, Phoebe thought wryly.

While she was in Midburton, she decided, she might as well do the rest of her shopping. It was an odd sensation actually having money in her pocket, for once, instead of having to count every penny.

The scent shop had special Christmas baskets

crammed
with bath foam, body lotions and other toiletries in exquisite old-fashioned fragrances like rose, lily and honeysuckle, and Phoebe chose one for Carrie.

For Lynn there was an array of the newest colours in nail enamels, prettily packaged.

In an art shop she found an enormous paintbox for Tara, with sensible sized brushes, and a thick pad of paper where she could create her masterpieces.

After all, she couldn't play with the dolls' house all day and every day during the long winter. She'd need some alternative form of interest.

But I won't be there to see it, Phoebe thought with a pang. I won't be there to supervise and praise her.

Only a short while before she'd been planning a new career—sorting out her life, her future.

Now, she knew, with pain, that everything she really wanted—all her happiness and true fulfilment—was in the house at Fitton Magna.

And she had to leave it behind.

She gave herself a mental shake, pushing her wretchedness to the back of her mind. It was still going to be Christmas very soon, and she had Dominic's present to buy. Even that presented a major problem. Any form of clothing, or even male toiletries, seemed too intimate somehow, unless she stuck to something safe but dull like socks and handkerchiefs, and they didn't appeal at all.

She wandered from shop to shop, examining and discarding, getting more and more low-spirited, until she came across a small, independent bookseller. On display in the window was a handsomely presented reprint of a pre-war local history book, wonderfully illustrated, with a big section on Fitton Magna and its environs.

Not too personal, but clearly specially chosen, Phoebe decided jubilantly, discovering that it was a limited edition produced by a local printer.

And even when she was long gone the book would

remain at the house, a tangible reminder that she had lived there. A remembrance of her, she thought wistfully.

The shop had some unusual wrapping paper and tags too, so, in spite of her emotional turmoil, Phoebe could feel well-satisfied with her efforts as she drove home.

She couldn't wait for Dominic to phone that night, and hovered expectantly for Tara to finish her conversation so that she could tell him, 'Mission accomplished'. But Tara came running back to inform her that Dominic had rung off without asking to speak to her.

'Oh,' Phoebe said blankly, feeling totally and absurdly put down.

'I think he was in a hurry. But he says he's coming back tomorrow night,' Tara added with delight, and Phoebe supposed she would have to make do with that.

The next twenty-four hours passed tranquilly enough, apart from Tara's unwillingness to go to school.

'It's boring,' she said rebelliously. 'All they do is practise the play, and I have to just sit there. And Judith, who got the part of the Virgin Mary, is *awful*,' she added broodingly.

Although sympathetic, Phoebe had to hide a smile. 'Why don't you write a nativity play of your own?' she suggested. 'Then we can all act it here.'

Tara's face lit up. 'With me as the Virgin Mary?'

'We wouldn't have anyone else,' Phoebe assured her.

'Daddy could be Joseph,' said the embryo playwright, 'and Carrie can be the innkeeper, and you can be all the shepherds.'

'Sounds good to me,' Phoebe agreed. 'But what do we do for the Wise Men?'

'We'll have to wait and see if Uncle Tony comes back,' said Tara.

God forbid, Phoebe thought devoutly.

Tony's unexpected intrusion into their lives lurked uneasily in the back of her mind, like an unanswered question. Or an unexploded bomb.

My first love, she thought with self-disgust. Only it was never love—merely infatuation. And how could I have been so blind—so self-delusional?

But she knew the answer to that. She hadn't known what love really was.

Not until now, she thought. Not until now.

It was late in the evening when Dominic finally returned. Tara, furious at not being allowed to stay up for him, had sulked her way to bed. And Carrie had turned down the oven for the rich beef casserole she'd prepared to the gentlest simmer, prophesying doom and disaster for it if he didn't come soon.

He looks tired, was Phoebe's first thought. And unhappy, too.

Perhaps his rescue plan had failed after all.

She followed him into the study. He paused in the act of unpacking his briefcase and looked at her, one brow lifted interrogatively.

No smile or word of greeting, she registered bleakly. She was wearing the moss-green needlecord shirtwaister that she'd bought during her expedition to Midburton. And suddenly she felt foolish, as if she'd dressed for a celebration only to find it cancelled.

She hurried into speech. 'I thought you'd want to know that I'm collecting Tara's present on Christmas Eve.' She could hear the nervousness in her own voice. 'I thought, if I brought it in by the kitchen entrance, I could hide it in the utility room. Tara never goes in there.'

He nodded curtly. 'Is she asleep?'

'No, she won't be. She's been excited all day, waiting for you.'

Soften, she thought pleadingly. Smile for me now.

But there was nothing. Dominic seemed to look through her. 'Then I'll go up to her.'

Phoebe went back to the drawing room. The bag with the little wooden dolls, the scraps of fabric and her sewing kit was safely hidden under one of the sofas. She retrieved it, and went on with the dress she was sewing for the female doll.

Something was clearly wrong, she thought, but what? He'd been so different when they'd spoken on the telephone—so much warmer, so much more human. But perhaps that was the problem. After all, he'd made it clear that there could never be anything between them. Maybe he regretted dropping his guard with her, even for a few moments, and many miles away, and this was his way of telling her.

Her sewing wasn't difficult work, but it was fiddly, requiring the kind of concentration she wasn't capable of just now, and she yelped as she jabbed the needle into her finger instead of the fabric, ruefully sucking away the spot of blood.

It would be best to abandon it for the evening and listen to the radio in her room, she decided dispiritedly. And she would be out of Dominic's way, as he clearly wished.

It was here that Carrie found her half an hour later.

'He's barely touched his dinner,' she said, pursing her lips. 'Now, he's having coffee in the study, and he wants to talk to you.'

Phoebe uncurled herself from the little armchair and stood up.

'Did he say what it was about?' she asked apprehensively.

Carrie shook her head. 'He isn't saying very much at all.' She sighed. 'This is how he was after—' She stopped, as if aware she was straying into indiscretion.

'After his marriage broke up?' Phoebe asked, wincing inwardly.

'Well—yes. And I thought he'd put all that behind him. That he was looking forward, not back.'

'That isn't always easy,' Phoebe said quietly, and went out of the room.

The study door was shut, so she tapped lightly, and waited.

'Come in.' His tone was short and uncompromising.

He was standing by the fire, looking down into the flames, one foot on the brass fender. He'd changed, she noticed, out of his dark City suit into jeans and a casual sweater.

'You wanted to see me?'

'Yes, there were a couple of things.' He paused. 'Firstly, I've written to Westcombe Park School, informing them that Tara won't be returning in the New Year.'

'Oh, that's good,' she said with relief. 'I'm sure it's absolutely the right decision.'

'You think so?' The grey eyes were remote. 'I can't say I've been too impressed with my own judgement lately.' There was another, longer pause. 'Look how wrong I've been about you,' he added with cold emphasis.

'I don't understand—' she began, but he interrupted derisively.

'Don't lie to me, Phoebe. And, more importantly, don't get my daughter to lie to me. Because that is unforgivable.'

She felt as if he'd struck her in the face. 'I haven't lied,' she said unevenly. 'And I don't believe Tara would either.'

'Neither did I.' His tone bit. 'That is until earlier this evening, when I asked her if Tony Cathery had been in this house and she swore he hadn't. Which, as we all know, is not the case. Is it, my innocent-eyed hypocrite?'

Shocked into silence, Phoebe could only stare at him.

'I can't dictate to you over your love life,' he went on grimly. 'Although I'd have thought previous experience would have taught you something. But I object to you carrying on your amours under my roof with that piece of scum. I'm sure I don't have to tell you why.' His mouth curled in distaste. 'No doubt you've been in his confidence all along—even six years ago.

'Until your advent, I'd managed to keep him out of my orbit. I genuinely believed that whatever relationship you'd had with him was long over. If I'd thought for one minute it was just on hold...' He drew a long, bitter breath.

'But dragging Tara into it. Forcing her to cover up for you. Trusting that bastard with her. Letting him drive her to school.' His voice thickened. 'My God, Phoebe, how could you do that?'

It was one terrible bombshell after another. Phoebe was reeling, her mind going crazy, but she had to get control—to defend herself somehow. Deal with the last accusation first, because that was in a minor league compared with everything else.

'You think he waited for my permission?' she demanded hotly. 'You must know him better than that. Tara wanted to go with him, and he drove off with her before I could stop him. What was I supposed to do—run after the car? As it was, I was just thankful that she got to school safely.'

'Amen to that.'

'As a matter of interest, how did you find out?'

'Unfortunately for you, Hazel was at the school for a governors' meeting, and she saw him drop Tara off. She could hardly believe her eyes.'

'Or wait to get on the phone, it seems,' Phoebe said acidly.

'She's an old friend,' he returned. 'Knowing the situation, she was naturally concerned. She acted with the best of intentions.'

'Of course.' Phoebe paused. 'Regarding the ''cover-up'', I admit that Carrie and I thought it would be better not to mention he'd been here.' She didn't look at him. 'Not to reopen old wounds. But not to lie about it either,' she added fiercely. 'That was never on the agenda. If you'd asked, we'd have told you. We—meant well, too.'

'So why was Tara so scared to speak?' he asked scornfully. 'Why was she sobbing in my arms just now, saying that she'd had to promise not to tell or her Christmas would be ruined? What kind of pressure is that to put on a child?'

'I never said anything like that. I wouldn't. I couldn't.' Phoebe beat a clenched fist into the palm of her other hand. 'And I'm not having an affair with Tony Cathery. If you won't take my word for it, ask Tara where I slept that night. And she'll tell you I was with her.'

The grey eyes narrowed. 'Then why did he come here—if not to see you? He knows he's not allowed anywhere near this place.'

'He walked in, claimed to be your stepbrother and made himself at home. Maybe you should have followed up your embargo by having the locks changed.' Phoebe paused. 'But he wasn't looking for me,' she added with stark emphasis. 'He was as surprised to see me as I was appalled to see him.'

'Do you think I'm a fool?' Dominic demanded contemptuously. 'Whatever motive could he have had? He was taking a hell of a risk. At our last meeting I swore I'd kill him if I ever saw him again.'

'Another excellent reason for keeping his presence quiet. And I'm the last person you should ask about Tony's motivation.'

He laughed harshly. 'You knew him very well six years ago.'

Phoebe shook her head. 'I never knew him at all. Not the real person—if there is one.' She took a deep, steadying breath. 'And while we're on the subject of deception—how long have you known? That it was me, I mean?'

His mouth twisted. 'Ever since the night you barged in, accusing me of being an uncaring father. Oh, there'd been some surface changes, of course. You were wearing clothes, and that bloody wig had gone. But you couldn't disguise your eyes.'

He threw his head back. 'That crushed, scared look you gave me as you came downstairs haunted me for a long time. And just for a moment I met it again, head-on, here in this room.'

He shrugged. 'And there was the name, as well. You don't encounter that many Phoebes in a lifetime.'

'No,' she said bitterly. 'I don't suppose you do. So, if you knew all along, why didn't you simply kick me into oblivion like last time?'

'Because I was intrigued.' His voice slowed to a drawl. 'From centrefold to uptight child-rights protestor seemed a hell of a transformation. And, as you so patently didn't want to be recognised, I decided to play along.'

She said tonelessly, 'Your family seems to specialise in games of one kind or another.'

'In which you were the first to join, remember?' The grey eyes glittered, stripping off the concealing lines of the moss-green dress. 'Tony told me what an eager volunteer you were. Always happier without your clothes than in them.'

'And you believed him?' She wrapped her arms defensively round her body.

'Backed up by the evidence of my own eyes, yes.' He was smiling now, his mouth curling in sensual reminiscence. 'He'd left me this note—"Many happy returns. Your birthday present is unwrapped on your bed". Even then, I didn't realise what he meant, until I opened the door and saw you there.'

He paused. 'And, for the record, don't think I wasn't tempted, darling.' He made the endearment sound like an insult. 'It had been a hell of a few weeks, and it might have been some small recompense to take Tony's woman as mindlessly as he'd taken mine. Although that wasn't the plan, naturally,' he added softly. 'I was supposed to react exactly as I did, and let you leave unscathed. Good old predictable Dominic.'

'Unscathed—is that what you think?' Her voice shook. 'My God, how little you know. I was humiliated—degraded. If you think your failure to attack me was some kind of let-off...'

Dominic laughed, the sound echoing harshly.

'Attack?' he jeered. 'I don't think I'd have been driven to that extreme. You may have chosen to shelter behind this demure façade, but you're fooling no one except yourself. I've held you, remember? And gauged the depths of your response. Or are you going to deny that too?'

She couldn't say anything. She couldn't speak or move. And she should run, because there was real danger here.

'No,' he went on softly. 'The real girl was there on my bed that night—warm, passionate and much more than willing. Would you like me to prove it to you?'

Two strides brought him to her. His arms went round her roughly, pulling her against him in a demand that brooked no denial. His kiss was hard, plundering all the sweetness of her mouth without mercy.

She couldn't breathe, or even think with any coherence, but the instinct to escape, before it was too late, was still strong. She tried to push him away, but his chest was like an iron wall against her frantic hands. She could feel the race of his heart under her fingers. Sense the aroused, desperate trembling of his flesh. And match it with her own shaken, reluctant excitement.

It was, she realised, indeed too late.

She felt herself sway in his embrace, and his clasp slackened a little—but only so that he could bend her backwards over his arm in a pliant arc, his lips trailing fire down the line of her throat while his hand moulded the softness of her breast with total and compelling assurance.

He undid the buttons on her dress, pushing the soft fabric off her shoulder, then sliding down her bra strap so that he could release her breast from the confines of its lacy cup.

Her flesh seemed to swell at his first touch on its nakedness, her nipple hardening in unresisting pleasure under the play of his skilful fingers.

She heard her own raw gasp of delight as he took the eager, dusky peak into his mouth, stroking it gently, subtly, with his tongue.

Her body was melting, imbued with a strange languor. When Dominic lifted her fully into his arms, she offered no protest, allowing him to carry her to the thick rug in front of the fireplace.

He lay beside her, framing her face with his hands as he kissed her again, gently this time, and very deeply. Then, without haste, he unclasped the belt of her dress and unfastened the remaining buttons. He raised her slightly so that he could free her arms from the sleeves, then unhooked her bra and tossed it aside.

He looked down at her, and she felt herself tremble under the intensity of his gaze.

He said quietly, 'I've dreamed of seeing you like this—touching you. You're like some pale, sweet rose made flesh.'

She felt his mouth burn swiftly and softly in the valley between her breasts, then his hands cupped each delicate mound in turn for the lingering adoration of his lips.

Through half-closed eyes, Phoebe saw the flames dance on the hearth behind him, and felt them riot in her blood. She too had dreamed, she thought hazily. Dreams she had never admitted even to herself—until now, when they were all coming true.

Dominic stroked her softly and sensually, smoothing his hand from her shoulder down to her thigh, making each inch of silky skin his own. She revelled in every tiny movement, feeling her body bloom under the brush of his fingers.

It was only when she felt the satin glide of his caress parting her thighs that she realised that the remainder of her clothing had been discarded, and she was naked.

No one had ever touched her so intimately before, and she whimpered softly and greedily, suffused in heated, molten pleasure. She was consumed by a yearning she hardly understood, her body moving in restless, questing delight under the tender expertise of his exploration of her.

Tiny waves of sensation were lapping at her, tingling along her limbs, shivering at her nerve-endings, intensifying under the sweet rhythm of his fingers to such a pitch that her entire being seemed to be focused on this tiny, elusive core of pleasure.

She was so close—dear God, so close.

'Don't stop—please.' She hardly recognised her own sobbing whisper.

'Never.'

She sensed the core inside her building up to some pinnacle, strained to reach it, and felt her body explode in unimaginable glory.

She came shuddering back to earth, and some measure of control, and found there were tears on her face. Dominic touched them with his lips.

'You're supposed to enjoy it,' he whispered, teasing her, and she smiled at him waveringly, wonderingly, because she had never known such rapture existed.

The sudden shrilling of the telephone was a raucous, jarring intrusion.

'Don't answer it.' Phoebe caught at his arm as he started to get to his feet.

'I must, or Carrie will be coming in to find out what's wrong.' He freed himself gently and went over to the desk.

He lifted the receiver and gave the number. Phoebe saw his face change as he listened.

She felt cold, suddenly, and oddly indecent, as if there were a third person actually in the room.

As she reached for her dress he said quietly, 'Good evening, Serena. To what do I owe this unexpected pleasure?'

Phoebe halted abruptly, staring at him in shock.

His brows drew together in a faint frown as he listened for what seemed an eternity.

'If that's what you wish,' he said at last, his tone expressionless, 'Tara will be delighted, naturally.' Another pause, then, 'Yes, of course. Goodnight.'

He replaced the receiver with great deliberation, then walked across the room and poured himself a drink.

'My former wife,' he said with precision, 'is coming to spend Christmas with us. I'd better break the news to Carrie.'

He looked down at Phoebe, still huddled on the rug, holding her dress against her, and his face was remote—a stranger's.

He said, 'I think, under the circumstances, you'd better get dressed—don't you?'

Then he swallowed his whisky, put down the glass and walked out of the room.

Leaving her there alone. And bereft.

CHAPTER TWELVE

'MY WISH came true,' Tara said buoyantly. 'Mummy's going to be here for Christmas.'

'Indeed she is.' Phoebe forced a smile. She felt totally bruised—traumatised by the events of the past twenty-four hours. But, she told herself bleakly, she had no one to blame but herself.

She couldn't even remember dragging on her clothes and escaping to her room last night. Yet she must have managed it somehow, because, at some time in the small hours, she'd become aware that she was lying, cold and shivering, on top of her bed, the pillow soaked with her tears.

She'd undressed and got under the covers, staring dry-eyed into the darkness, trying to come to terms with what had happened and failing miserably.

She'd behaved like a fool—worse than a fool. She'd fallen headlong into Dominic's arms, bewitched by his kisses, seduced by his caresses. She'd put her mind on hold and let her senses take over. And now she had to endure the consequences.

Some time, during the course of the day, she would have to face him. To know that he was remembering, as she was, the totality of her surrender. That she'd more than justified his opinion of her. *Warm and willing*, she thought, and shuddered.

And how would he ever believe that it was only *his* lips and *his* hands which could have swept away her defences? That she'd given herself because she loved him, and love created trust?

But he wouldn't have to believe it, she reminded herself painfully. Nor would he want to. He'd engineered that little bout of lovemaking to prove a point. Nothing more. He'd made no promises. Offered no commitment. And once the encounter was over, and the real world had jogged his consciousness, he'd walked away without a backward glance.

And now I have to deal with the real world, too, she acknowledged with a small, inward sigh. Which is taking Tara to school, and coping with her understandable excitement about her mother. Even if I can't share it.

'Is Daddy cross with me?' Tara asked.

'No, why should he be?' Phoebe braked gently for a set of traffic lights.

'Because I had to fib to him about Uncle Tony,' Tara said in a small voice. 'I didn't want to, but Uncle Tony said I mustn't say a word about him being here or he'd stop Mummy coming to see me. And Daddy kept asking and asking me.'

'Listen, poppet,' Phoebe said gently, 'I think it would be an excellent plan to put Uncle Tony out of your mind for good. He had no right to ask you to tell fibs, and Daddy would be cross with him rather than you, so don't worry any more.'

'All right.' Tara brightened again. 'I wonder how soon Mummy will be here?'

'Too soon for me,' Carrie said bluntly, dealing briskly with the potatoes for lunch. 'I can't understand Mr Dominic agreeing to let her come here.'

'It's just for Tara,' Phoebe offered. 'Serena Vane is her mother after all.'

Carrie snorted. 'A farmyard cat's a better mother than that madam's ever been,' she said grimly. 'No, she'll be up to something, mark my words.' She filled the pan with water and placed it on the stove. 'But every cloud has its silver lining,' she went on. 'I know one nose that'll be out of joint.'

And I know another, thought Phoebe, staring out over the rainswept orchard.

Lunch over, she had another go at dressing Tara's dolls. She was sitting in the drawing room, head bent, absorbed in tacking together a tiny pair of cord trousers, when a slight sound made her glance up.

Dominic was standing in the doorway, watching her. Phoebe looked back at him, aware that a blush she couldn't control was bathing her entire body in heat. She put down her sewing, before she yielded to temptation and stabbed herself through the heart with the needle.

'Did you want to speak to me about something?' Formality was the keynote, she told herself. Behave as if last night was just a figment of the imagination.

'There are things that need to be said.' He paused. 'About last night...'

Phoebe's hands twisted together in her lap so tightly that her knuckles ached. So much, she thought, for good intentions.

'There's nothing to discuss.' There was a slight huskiness in her voice. 'You set out to prove something, and you succeeded. I have zero will-power, just as you said. Now, can we forget the whole embarrassing episode?'

'It's not that simple.'

'Why not? I'm hardly going to sue you for sexual harassment. And I don't intend to swap girlish confidences with Miss Vane either.'

'How very reassuring.' His tone had an edge to it. 'For God's sake, Phoebe, can't you see how impossible the whole situation is?'

'Do you want me to go and pack?' She hadn't thought she could hurt so much, and live.

He bit his lip. 'No—at least, not yet. I feel we should let our current arrangement stand. Unless, of course, you feel you must...?'

'No.' She stretched her lips in a smile. 'I—I'll stay until the New Year, as I promised. And you don't have to worry. I don't need any further demonstrations of how stupid I can be.'

'Phoebe, for God's sake.' He sounded raw.

'I've also found out why Tara lied about Tony,' she went on, as if he hadn't spoken. 'He put pressure on her. Claimed he could cancel her mother's visit if she gave him away.'

Dominic frowned. 'But Tara didn't know her mother was coming. Not until I told her so this morning.'

'Actually, she did. She mentioned the possibility to me way back, although I think she'd rather lost faith in it latterly.'

'I should have known,' he said grimly. 'Serena does so little on impulse.' He paused. 'It seems I owe you an apology—one of several.'

'No,' she said quickly. 'That's—all right.' Don't say you're sorry you touched me, she pleaded silently. Oh, please don't say that. 'If it's any consolation, Tara hated doing it,' she added.

He said bleakly, 'When I'm ready to be consoled, I'll bear it in mind.'

There was a blast of cold, damp air sweeping into the house as the front door opened suddenly.

From the hall, Hazel Sinclair called impatiently, 'Dominic? Dom, darling, where are you?'

Dominic turned towards the door, but before he could head her off she was in the room.

'I saw your car on the drive.' Smiling, she advanced on him, holding out her hands, encouraging him to kiss her on both cheeks, Continental-style. 'You didn't let me know you were home, bad boy. I thought, as I was passing, I should drop off these tickets for the school Christmas show. It's next Wednesday,' she continued vivaciously. 'Carols, solo items, a nativity play, and mince pies and punch afterwards.'

'That's kind of you,' he said politely. 'But I don't think we can make it.'

'Oh, darling...' She drawled the word to three times its normal length. 'You're not sulking, are you, because your Tara didn't get the lead?'

He gave her a meditative look. 'You know about that, do you?'

'Well, naturally. I am a governor, after all. And I gather Mary Poppins over there did make some kind of fuss. She really shouldn't interfere in the school's internal affairs.'

'Well, it won't be necessary for much longer,' Dominic said pleasantly. 'I'm enrolling Tara at Fitton Magna Primary School next year. I don't really care for Westcombe Park's internal affairs either.'

Hazel's laugh held no amusement. 'You do know you're being quite absurd? The whole thing's a storm in a teacup. Tara can't expect to be favoured because of her mother.'

'Indeed not, but I don't think favour comes into it. She's been deliberately excluded from the entire production.'

'I'm sure there's a very good reason.'

'Perhaps you'd like to tell me what it is?'

She shrugged. 'How on earth would I know?'

'You don't like Tara, do you, Hazel? You were very angry the other day when she called you a name. This wouldn't be your revenge, by any chance?'

'I hope,' Hazel said with dignity, 'that I'm not that petty.'

'I hope so too,' Dominic returned civilly, 'but I'm not convinced.'

'Dominic, darling.' She tried to laugh, but it didn't quite work. 'I can't believe we're having this conversation. You're—almost being insulting. Now, we'll forget all this nonsense and we'll go to the show together on Wednesday. And, to prove there are no hard feelings, I'll talk to Mrs Franks. Tara can play one of the villagers.'

He shook his head. 'I'm sorry, Hazel, but Serena will be here, and Tara will want to spend her time with her mother.'

'Serena.' The name was choked out of her. 'What are you talking about?'

He shrugged. 'She's coming here for Christmas.'

'And you're letting her—after everything that's happened?' Her voice rose almost to a shriek. 'You must be mad.'

'Tara resides with me, but Serena is allowed access,' he said levelly. 'She's choosing to exercise that right over Christmas. I'd need a damned good reason to stop her.'

'But you've got one,' she said eagerly. 'We've been invited skiing, remember? We can fit Tara in somewhere...'

Phoebe tried to shrink under the sofa cushions. Oh, God, she thought. This is awful.

'As one of the villagers?' Dominic asked with irony. He shook his head again. 'It isn't going to happen, Hazel, but I'm sure you won't lack for company.'

For a moment, Phoebe thought Hazel was going to lose it completely, and braced herself for the explosion.

Then the other woman turned, and almost flung herself out of the room. A moment later they heard the roar of her car engine, and the splutter of gravel as she took off.

'That,' remarked Phoebe 'wasn't very kind.'

His face was wintry. 'Perhaps I'm not feeling very kind. But, considering the way she's treated Tara, it was benevolence itself. Even telling me she'd seen Tony at the school was an attempt to make trouble.'

'You can't be sure of that,' Phoebe protested.

'I can,' he said. 'As I've told you, I've known Hazel for a long time. It didn't work between us then, and it never will. And now, of course, everything's changing anyway.'

'Why?'

'Because Serena's coming back.' His tone was matter-of-fact.

Phoebe stowed her bag of sewing back under the sofa. 'It's time I fetched Tara,' she said, and left.

She actually arrived at the school gates with five minutes to spare, and settled down to read her book while she waited, until disturbed by a peremptory rap on the driver's window.

She looked round, and saw, with a sinking heart, Hazel Sinclair glaring in at her. Reluctantly, she wound down the window.

'I suppose you think you've been very clever,' Hazel said thickly.

'You couldn't be more wrong,' Phoebe returned with total sincerity.

'You may think you've wormed your way into Dominic's life, but you won't have a prayer once Serena gets to work.' The other woman's tone was vicious. 'He's never got over what she did to him. He can't handle a serious relationship with anyone else when he's still carrying a torch for her. That divorce is in name only, and you'd better believe it.'

Phoebe prayed that no trace of her inner pain was showing on her face. 'Thanks for the warning,' she said. 'But it's not necessary. I'm the nanny, and nothing else. I'm there just for Tara.'

'You look ever so funny,' Tara said, climbing into the car a few minutes later. 'Are you going to be sick?'

'Not until after Christmas,' said Phoebe, and started the engine.

Serena Vane arrived the following Tuesday. Phoebe, despising herself for her own curiosity, watched the chauffeur-driven limousine draw up on the gravel.

The chauffeur came round to open the rear passenger door and Serena Vane got out, slowly and gracefully.

She was taller than Phoebe had realised, with a mane of reddish-blonde hair. She was wearing a coat in supple cream suede, with boots to match.

Serena stood, looking appraisingly up at the house, and, though Phoebe knew she could not be seen, she shrank further behind the sheltering curtain.

The chauffeur was taking things from the car—a set of Louis Vuitton cases, and, incongruously, a large cardboard box with carrying handles. Miss Vane directed him to carry it all into the house, and walked ahead of him up the steps and out of sight.

Phoebe gave a small, unhappy sigh, and went to sit at the nursery table with her book. Whatever kind of family reunion would now be taking place downstairs, she wasn't expected to be part of it.

It was nearly an hour before Carrie, po-faced, came to fetch her.

'She wants to meet you. She's all sweetness and light, and I wouldn't trust her as far as I could throw her. She's brought Tara a puppy, of all things, and it's piddled in the hall already,' she added darkly.

It was Dominic whom Phoebe looked for first when she entered the drawing room. He was standing beside the fireplace, his expression unreadable but his eyes fixed unwinkingly on his former wife. A golden Labrador puppy was asleep at his feet.

Serena Vane was ensconced on one of the sofas, with Tara adoringly at her side. The coat had been removed to reveal an equally expensive cream bouclé dress. Her lips and nails were painted an exotic deep crimson, and the eyes which examined Phoebe were so dark a blue as to seem almost black.

'So you're Phoebe,' said the lovely voice. 'You're the kind girl who's been taking care of my greatest treasure. I simply can't thank you enough. It's so dreadful, being thousands of miles away and imagining her with strangers.'

'It—it must be,' Phoebe stammered, feeling totally banal.

Dominic said, 'Shall I ask Carrie to bring in tea for us all?'

Serena laughed up at him. 'Tea, darling? Don't say there's no champagne to welcome me home.' She gazed round the room, giving a rapturous sigh. 'Oh, I've been away far too long.' She gave Tara a quick hug. 'But Mummy's back now, sweetie. And everything's going to be all right.'

She gave Dominic another swift smile. 'And you don't have to worry about Christmas; I've got it all arranged. I've ordered everything and they're bringing it later this afternoon. A tree, food, wine—everything.'

'But we've got a tree,' Tara pointed out, puzzled.

'Yes, sweetie, I noticed.' The lopsided angel was sent a disparaging look. 'But wait until you see the one I've bought. I'm sure we can find somewhere else for that one,' she added dismissively.

'And Carrie's done all the food,' Tara went on.

'Sweetie.' Serena's voice became slightly metallic. 'Don't keep trying to spoil all Mummy's lovely surprises, or I shall be sorry I came.' She paused. 'Would you like to see what else I've brought you?'

'We usually exchange presents on Christmas morning,' Dominic put in quietly.

'Oh, I can't wait that long.' Serena pointed to a large flat box tied with ribbons. 'It's in there.'

'It' turned out to be a fun fur coat. Watching Tara parade up and down in it obediently, Phoebe decided it was tacky and hateful, then berated herself for being a bitch.

The puppy decided to wake up, and began to wander round the room.

'He wants to go out,' Dominic said abruptly. 'Come on, Tara, we'll take him into the garden. Carrie won't want any more messes in the house.'

'Poor Carrie,' Serena said as the door closed behind them. 'I wonder if she's still adequate for the job.'

'Very much so,' Phoebe returned evenly.

'Well, I shall have to judge that for myself.' She glanced round. 'Heaven knows when this room was decorated last. I shall have to take the entire house in hand.'

'Over Christmas?' Phoebe asked in bewilderment. 'I know it's different in the States, but here everything closes down until New Year.'

'Then I shall just have to be patient.' Serena leaned back against the cushions, crossing her endless legs. 'But I've got plenty of time.' The crimson lips parted to reveal perfect teeth. 'I told Dominic I was coming for Christmas, but that isn't strictly true. I've had a lot of time to think things over, and I've decided that we should reconcile—for Tara's sake.'

Phoebe felt as if a hand had closed round her throat and was squeezing the life out of her. But her voice sounded surprisingly normal. 'Does Mr Ashton know this?'

'Not yet.' Serena stretched languidly, full breasts thrusting against the bouclé dress. 'Actually I thought I'd tell him tonight—in bed. That's always the best time.'

The dark blue eyes swept over Phoebe. 'Now go and find some champagne, will you, dear? I want to celebrate.'

The lopsided angel's bearing had not improved during her transfer to the nursery, Phoebe thought sadly as she made sure the fir tree was secure in its pot, before she went to bed.

During the afternoon, two vans blazoned with the names of famous London stores had arrived, and Serena's Christmas had been duly unloaded, to Tara's bewilderment and Carrie's silent outrage.

As a consequence, the drawing room was now occupied by a six-foot, glittering artificial tree, a symphony in gold and silver.

During dinner, Serena had turned up her nose at the beautifully roasted haunch of venison, protesting that nearly everyone was turning to vegetarianism these days.

But not teetotalism apparently, Phoebe thought drily, having observed how much champagne the lovely Serena had put away.

She had also noticed how totally absorbed Dominic seemed in his ex-wife. How his eyes never seemed to leave her for a moment. The idea of a reconciliation was becoming less absurd by the minute.

He's like a puppet, Phoebe told herself unhappily. All she has to do is twitch the strings.

The final straw came when Phoebe went into the drawing room after dinner and found a tell-tale pile of chewed wood and torn fabric on the rug. The puppy had unearthed her sewing from beneath the sofa and destroyed Tara's dolls. Phoebe could have wept as she hastily bundled the damp scraps onto the back of the fire before Tara, who'd been allowed to stay up for dinner, saw them.

All in all, it's been one hell of a day, she thought wretchedly, turning off the nursery light.

She looked in on Tara before she went to her own room. The little girl had become horrendously overexcited, had made a scene about the puppy not being allowed to sleep in her room and had had to be dissuaded from wearing her fun fur to bed. But now she was fast asleep.

I ought to feel glad for her, Phoebe thought, a lump in her throat. This is what she's always wanted—her mother and father together again. But I can't. I can't...

There was another irritation when she arrived in her room and discovered she'd left her bag, and the book she was reading, downstairs in the small sitting room, where she'd spent the rest of the evening, having decided she could take no more 'happy families' in the drawing room.

At first she determined to do without them. But it was unlikely she would get to sleep immediately, she realised. She had far too much on her mind.

I'll go downstairs and fetch them, she decided, tightening the sash of her robe.

Moving quietly on slippered feet, she descended the stairs to the main landing and paused in the dim light, hearing a door open somewhere.

Serena Vane came out of her room. She was wearing a totally sheer black chiffon nightdress which displayed every curve of her perfect body.

Standing in the shadows, Phoebe watched her cross to Dominic's door, turn the handle quietly and slip inside.

The reconciliation, she thought numbly, was complete.

CHAPTER THIRTEEN

'SOMETIMES,' said Serena, directing a misty look at the camera, 'it takes time to establish where one's true priorities are. I'm just thankful I found out before it was too late.'

The television crew from the local station had taken over the house early that morning, and now the recorded interview was in full swing.

The attractive brunette who was asking the questions looked down at her notes. 'Does this mean you'll be pursuing your career in this country from now on, Miss Vane?'

'I'm considering a number of options,' Serena said softly. 'But I haven't ruled out a return to Hollywood.'

'Even though you've been sacked from *Heart of Steel*?'

'I'm afraid you've been misinformed.' Whatever the state of her heart, there was a note of steel in Serena's voice. 'The director and I had artistic differences, but our parting was a mutual decision, and perfectly amicable.'

'And your relationship with Bryn Stratton—was that an amicable parting too?'

Serena smiled sadly. 'Bryn will always be a very dear friend, and on that basis we're still in touch. Shall we leave it at that?'

The interviewer smiled back. 'So you're aware that he's been booked into a Beverly Hills clinic for drug and alcohol abuse?'

Serena's pause was fractionally too long. 'As his friend, I prefer not to discuss his problems.'

So she didn't know, thought Phoebe, who was trying to be unobtrusive at the back of the room, and keep an eye on a bored and miserable Tara at the same time.

They'd had over a week of interviews, from Fleet Street tabloids to the local weekly paper, and each time Tara had been trotted out for the photographs in one of the lace-trimmed dresses that Serena had brought with her for the purpose.

Even Dominic had appeared in a couple of them, Phoebe reflected unhappily. He'd stood unsmilingly on the steps while Serena clung to his arm.

Serena had come home because she couldn't bear to be parted from her little girl any longer, was the message being peddled, and this was the first time it had been really called into question. Festival TV seemed to have done their homework.

'And you're staying with your ex-husband over Christmas—isn't that rather unusual?'

Serena shrugged. 'Christmas is a time for families. Where a child is concerned, one must forget past, foolish differences.' Her smile became radiant. 'As far as I'm concerned, I've simply come home.'

The interviewer looked at Tara, who was sitting next to her mother and looking uncomfortable in a black velvet dress with a pleated muslin collar.

'And what about you, Tara? Are you going to be an actress like your mother?'

'Mummy says I am,' said Tara. 'She says I'm going to have a film test.'

The journalist's eyes flicked back to Serena. 'Is that so? Is Tara going to be the new child-star sensation?'

Serena's laugh was melodious. 'Oh, she's far too young to be considering anything like that. I want her to have a happy, untrammelled childhood.'

'But you said...' Tara began, then subsided as the protective maternal arm tightened around her shoulders and the interview was wound up.

Serena snapped her fingers imperiously in Phoebe's direction. 'Have the coffee served, will you?' she said, rising from the sofa and marching over to embark on a low-voiced but clearly furious argument with the show's producer.

'So what part do you play in this touching domestic drama?'

Phoebe, pouring coffee, turned to see the interviewer, Jilly Mason, smiling at her.

'Very minor,' she returned constrainedly. 'I'm Tara's nanny.'

'Rather you than me,' Jilly said candidly. 'A mate of mine worked on the publicity for your boss's last film and says no salary is worth it. I must say she got up my nose, too. This was supposed to be just a heart-warming piece about family reunions at Christmas.' She paused. 'Is her husband really taking her back?' she asked, too casually. 'I note he's not around today.'

'As I said, I'm just the nanny,' Phoebe returned, tight-lipped. 'I don't pry into my employers' affairs.'

'You don't need to pry to know about dear Serena's affairs,' Jilly said lightly. 'They've been well documented. Among her other pretty ways, of course. My friend says the studio have had enough, and the Snow Queen will never work in Hollywood again. But the little girl's a different matter. I reckon Serena sees her as a blank cheque.'

She walked away to talk to the cameraman, leaving Phoebe to stare after her with sudden uneasiness.

'I hate this dress,' Tara said, throwing the black velvet onto the bed and clambering back into jeans and sweatshirt. 'It itches. And I hate having my picture taken all the time. It's boring.'

'Any more grumbles to get off your chest?' Phoebe asked mildly, brushing the child's tumbled curls, and Tara pondered for a moment.

'Why is Mummy so cross sometimes?'

'I'm sure she doesn't mean to be,' Phoebe soothed, although, if she was honest, Serena's mercurial temperament was driving the whole household up the wall.

Except Dominic, of course, she reminded herself painfully. Maybe the passionate nights made up for the violent mood swings in the daytime.

Although he doesn't see many of them, she thought, because he's at work. And she's always calmed down and all smiles when he comes home in the evening.

Tara's lips trembled. 'She's going to be even crosser because I talked about the film test. It's supposed to be a big secret.'

Is it? Phoebe thought, biting her lip. And why is that, I wonder?

Aloud, she said, calmly, 'Then it's a pity you find photographs boring. If you're going to be in films, the camera will be on you all the time.' She paused. 'Are you sure that's what you want?'

Tara wrinkled her nose pensively. 'I don't want to leave you and Daddy.'

'Well, that's not likely to happen. The law says you have to stay with Daddy.'

'But when he and Mummy get married again, she'll be able to take me back to California. She said so.'

Phoebe swallowed. 'Well, yes,' she said slowly. 'I—I suppose she will.'

'Will you and Daddy come with us?' Tara asked anxiously. 'And what's going to happen to Muggins?'

'Muggins will stay here with Carrie,' Phoebe said reassuringly. 'He'll have learned to behave by then.'

The puppy had continued to cause chaos in the house. Newspapers and magazines were regularly shredded, the lower branches of Serena's gold and silver tree were looking threadbare and bedraggled, and he'd chewed through the flex of the fairy lights.

'Pity they weren't on,' Dominic had commented caustically.

But Muggins' nadir had been finding its way into Serena's bedroom—in which she still maintained a presumably token presence—and destroying her cream suede boots.

Oblivious to the fact that she'd introduced the vandal into the house, Serena had hysterically demanded that the puppy be put down, while Tara, in floods of tears, had begged for his life.

'Oh, God,' Dominic had said wearily, caught in the middle. 'I suppose I'll have to take him in hand.'

Which was why Muggins now accompanied Dominic to the office each day, and was learning a more responsible attitude to life.

When Phoebe and Tara went downstairs the television crew had gone, and so, apparently, had Serena, in a taxi and a temper, to do some shopping.

'Why didn't she ask me to go with her?' Tara asked woefully.

The million-dollar question, Phoebe thought bitterly. For a woman with a new-found dedication to her only child, Serena seemed to spend the minimum of time in her company. And surely she'd exhausted the attractions of Westcombe and Midburton as shopping centres by now.

She smiled down at the little girl. 'Because she knew I was going to take you out to pick some holly,' she said. 'Run and find your boots.'

They spent a muddy, hilarious afternoon, and came home with the car boot full. In addition, at Tara's insistence, Phoebe had called at the garden centre and bought some mistletoe.

Serena had returned by the time they reached home, and, Carrie informed them grimly, was resting and didn't want to be disturbed.

Phoebe occupied the time until supper by decorating

the hall and dining room, with Tara's eager assistance. The mistletoe was hung ceremoniously from the central chandelier in the hall.

'Does that look all right?' Phoebe asked, descending from her ladder.

'It looks magnificent,' Dominic said from the front doorway. The shuttered look that Phoebe had grown used to was gone, and he was smiling.

'Daddy—Daddy.' Tara was dancing with excitement. 'Phoebe's under the mistletoe. You've got to kiss her.'

'Here, then.' Dominic handed his daughter the lead, with a frantically squirming Muggins at the end of it, and walked to Phoebe, who was rooted to the spot. 'Sorry about this,' he murmured. 'But rules are rules.'

His hands closed on her shoulders and he drew her forward. His skin smelt cold and fresh, but it warmed every fibre of her being as she went into his arms. His lips were cool too, and infinitely tender, but there was none of the passion he'd once showed her.

He had made his choice, she realised, standing passively in his embrace. And this was his way of saying goodbye. And, oh, dear God, how could she bear it?

'Kissing the staff, sweetie? How very feudal.' Serena came slowly down the stairs. She was wearing a lounging robe, the colour of ripe cranberries, and her hair was loose on her shoulders. Shopping seemed to have put her in a better mood, because her eyes were brilliant, although the expression in them when she looked at Phoebe was far from friendly.

'A grand old tradition.' Dominic released Phoebe without particular haste.

'Does it include wives?' Serena reverted to playfulness. As Phoebe stepped back Serena came up to Dominic, sliding her arms round his neck and thrusting her hips forward against his.

This was not something Phoebe wanted to watch.

'Suppertime,' she said, and led Tara away.

* * *

Christmas Eve at last, Phoebe thought wearily as she parked the car at the rear of the precinct. And soon she'd be able to count her remaining days as a nanny on the fingers of one hand.

Quite apart from her emotional involvement, she would be thankful to leave.

Serena's attitude—while never cordial after the opening gush—had deteriorated fast after she'd caught Phoebe under the mistletoe with Dominic.

Phoebe was left in no doubt that she was an enemy, and therefore to be subjected to all the petty tyrannies that a fertile mind could invent. And Serena Vane was incredibly inventive.

The barrage of small unkindnesses, and snide, contemptuous remarks, seemed unending. Even Tara was the target for some of it, as punishment for the affection in which she obviously held Phoebe.

It was a ghastly situation.

Phoebe pinned on a smile as she went into the craft shop.

'I've come for the dolls' house and furniture.'

'Oh, yes, of course—for Mr Ashton. It's all packed up ready. Shall I help you carry it out to the car?'

'Oh, please,' Phoebe accepted gratefully.

'I do hope the little girl likes it,' the woman remarked as they manoeuvred the heavy carton into the back of the car. 'What a wonderful Christmas she's going to have—with her mother at home.'

'Wonderful,' Phoebe agreed levelly. 'I'm sure Tara will be in after Christmas to choose some more furniture.'

The other woman's eyes lit up. 'Oh, do you think Miss Vane will bring her? It would be so marvellous to meet her. We've seen such a lot of her since she came back—just in passing, of course.'

'Really?'

The other woman nodded vigorously. 'She calls in at

the perfume shop several times a week. As a matter of fact she was there earlier this morning.'

Phoebe's brows lifted. As far as she knew, Serena Vane, who rarely got up before noon, was still in her room. Or Dominic's room, she amended with an inward sigh.

'Are you quite sure?'

'Of course.' The other woman bridled slightly. 'I'd know her anywhere, and so would Marjorie, who helps me. And the taxi waiting at the end of the precinct, same as always. It was definitely her.'

'What a pity I didn't know. I could have offered her a lift.' *And been turned down with some unpleasant comment, no doubt.*

'I hope I haven't given her away,' the woman said archly. 'Perhaps it was your present she was buying.'

Phoebe forced another smile. 'I don't think so,' she said, and got into the car.

When she arrived at the house, she drove round to the back. She'd have to leave the dolls' house in the car, she decided, and ask Dominic to help with it later, when Tara was in bed.

As she went indoors she heard total uproar coming from the small sitting room. Serena Vane was shouting, and Tara was crying loudly.

Phoebe walked into the room. Tara was sitting at the piano, her face wet with tears, and Serena was looming over her.

'God-awful row,' she yelled. 'Hellish din, over and over again. Don't you know any other bloody tunes?'

Tara saw Phoebe and ran to her, burying her face in her stomach.

'It was my surprise,' she wailed. 'I was practising my surprise again, so that I could play it for everyone tomorrow, and Mummy was angry.'

Phoebe looked at Serena over Tara's head. 'What the hell's the matter with you?' she asked raggedly, her disgust with the older woman and her compassion for Tara outweighing her normal discretion. 'Did you have to ruin it for her?'

'*Ruin?*' Serena screeched, her face mottled with rage. 'I'm the one who's had her morning ruined. I've had this terrible migraine ever since I woke this morning. I haven't been able to raise my head from the pillow, and all I could hear was that ghastly tune. It's been driving me mad.'

'Then it's a pity you didn't stay in Midburton,' Phoebe said icily.

'What are you talking about? I've not been out of my room until this moment. I've been too ill.'

She certainly didn't look well. Her face was haggard and her eyes were dull.

'Miss Vane, you were seen by some people in an adjoining shop.' Phoebe stroked Tara's hair, feeling the sobs die away to hiccups.

'You lying bitch,' Serena said thickly. 'I tell you I haven't left the house.'

'Which makes you the liar, Miss Vane, not me.' Phoebe faced her steadily. 'But you're not just a liar. You're a cruel, heartless woman. Jilly Mason was right when she called you the Snow Queen.'

'What did you say?' Serena's voice rose to a scream, and she lunged forward and slapped Phoebe hard across the face.

Tara screamed. 'No,' she protested frantically. 'Don't hurt Phoebe, Mummy, please.'

'And you shut your damned face as well,' Serena gritted as Phoebe put up a numb hand to her reddening cheek.

'What the hell's going on here?' Dominic appeared in the doorway, removing his Barbour jacket.

'Phoebe and Mummy had a fight, and Mummy hit her.' Tara sounded terrified.

Phoebe crouched down beside her. 'Darling,' she whispered, 'I'm not hurt—I'm fine, really.'

Dominic turned to Serena, his brows lifting. 'Is this true?'

'She was appallingly, viciously rude,' Serena returned. 'I think your past attentions have gone to her head. Anyway, she's not staying in this house a moment longer. Get rid of her.'

There was a silence, longer than eternity, then Dominic turned towards Phoebe. His face was like stone.

'Is there somewhere you can go?' he asked with remote formality.

'No, Daddy,' Tara burst out urgently. 'It wasn't Phoebe's fault.'

He touched Tara's cheek gently. 'Quiet, darling. Go and find Carrie, and I'll deal with this.' As the child left the room, crying again, he looked at Phoebe. 'Well?'

'I can phone Lynn,' she said, dry-mouthed. 'Her family offered to have me ages ago. The invitation may still be open.'

'Then will you do so, please? Then pack. I'll drive you to Westcombe.'

'Get her a taxi—or let her walk,' said Serena.

Dominic took Serena's arm. 'This must have been terrible for you,' he said quietly. 'Why don't you go upstairs and rest?'

'Yes,' she said, staring around her almost unseeingly. 'Darling Dominic, you always know what's best for me.'

He put an arm round her, steadying her. His voice was gentle. 'Perhaps, at last, I'm learning,' he said, and led her from the room.

Lynn, though naturally curious, said yes without hesitation, so there was nothing for Phoebe to do but pack her few possessions into carrier bags.

Dominic was waiting in the hall when she came downstairs.

'Am I allowed to say goodbye to Tara?' she asked, her voice shaking a little.

'It's better you don't, I think. She's been through enough emotional traumas for one day.'

'I see.' She swallowed. 'How much did you hear?'

'Almost all of it.'

And you still blame me, she thought bitterly. She must have you in thrall.

'Before I forget,' she said as they entered Westcombe after a silent journey. 'The dolls' house is in the car.'

'Thank you.'

She directed him to Lynn's and he pulled up outside.

'Well—goodbye,' she forced through frozen lips. 'I'm sorry it had to end like this.'

'So am I,' he said sombrely. 'You don't know how sorry. But there is no other way.'

He pulled her into his arms and kissed her once, so hard that her mouth felt bruised. Then he leaned across, releasing her seat-belt and the catch on the passenger door.

'I have to get back,' he said.

Phoebe stood on the pavement, watching the Range Rover turn the corner and vanish. The door behind her opened, and Lynn and her mother appeared, waving to her excitedly.

Phoebe smiled back, and, moving like an automaton, walked up the path to face the loneliest, most desolate Christmas of her life.

She couldn't let her feelings show, of course. She told them simply that she'd had a row with Serena and been fired, making a joke of it.

And apparently she wasn't the only one. Mrs Preston had come to the end of her tether with Debbie, too, and Phoebe's old job was available at the café.

It wasn't ideal, but it was better than nothing, she thought.

She helped Mrs Fletcher make mince pies, watched a film on television without seeing one frame of it, and accompanied them all to the midnight service.

It was only when the children's choir sang 'Away in a Manger' that she found the tears coursing uncontrollably down her face.

And, bowing her head, she prayed that little Tara would have a merry Christmas, and that Dominic would find happiness with the woman he loved.

'We're going to take the presents round to my grandparents,' Lynn said the following morning. 'You're welcome to come.'

'It's all right. I'll stay and keep an eye on the turkey,' Phoebe returned, smiling resolutely.

'We won't be long.' Lynn gave her a narrow look. 'Sure you're OK?'

'I'm fine.' Phoebe pushed her towards the door. 'Go and play Santa Claus.'

Say after me, Phoebe Grant, she told herself sternly once she was alone—I'm *not* going to ruin the Fletchers' Christmas. I am *not* going to be a spectre at the feast.

She switched on the television, but all the programmes seemed to be about loved ones being reunited with each other over vast distances, and she couldn't bear it.

Fitton Magna wasn't a great distance, but it might as well have been the North Pole.

She put on a tape of some Christmas music, and settled down to read the book Lynn had bought her.

The sound of the key in the front door made her jump.

'That was quick—' she began, and stopped. Because it wasn't Lynn, or her parents, who appeared in the sitting room doorway, but Dominic.

He looked pale, and strained, and there were deep shadows under his eyes, but his smile touched her like a caress. Wordlessly, he held his arms out, and she went to him, half-stumbling.

He lifted her off her feet, kissing her deeply, hungrily, and for a delirious moment she responded with equal ardour. Then she remembered, and pushed him away.

'We mustn't.' Her voice trembled. 'This isn't right.'

He set her gently on her feet. 'It feels right to me, my love.'

'Please, don't say that,' she whispered. 'Aren't things bad enough already?'

'I'd say they were improving by the moment.'

'Is this why you sent me away?' she demanded with sudden fierceness. 'To hide me from Serena—so that I can be your bit on the side? Well, I won't. However much I love you, I won't live like that.'

'I certainly sent you away from Serena,' Dominic said mildly. 'But solely for your own protection. She was in a bloody dangerous mood. She'd already hit you, and I couldn't risk what she might do next, so I got you out of the house. It was clear she saw you as her rival, and I thought she might be easier to deal with if you weren't around.'

'Deal with?' Phoebe echoed in bewilderment. 'But you're remarrying.'

'No,' he said. 'Under no circumstances would I ever allow Serena past the margin of my life ever again.'

'But you were sleeping together.'

'Never,' he said. 'I admit she let me know she was available, but I wasn't. Do you really think I'd have laid a hand on her again after everything that's happened? After you?'

'Dominic—I saw her go into your room that first night.'

'Did she?' His brows lifted. 'How disappointing for her, my darling. Because I wasn't there. I went for a long drive, then sat on a hill and watched the dawn, and did a lot of thinking, and she certainly wasn't there when I got back.'

'But you must have some feelings for her still.' She found herself remembering Hazel Sinclair's bitter words.

'She's Tara's mother, and there's nothing I can do about that,' he said slowly. 'But my overriding feeling is pity, because she's screwed up her entire life. But that doesn't mean I'd let her screw up mine.'

'Then why did you let her come back?'

'To find out what she wanted. I knew she'd been sacked by the studio because I've had someone keeping an eye on her out there. I knew too that she'd broken with Bryn Stratton. He was the reason I was able to get custody of Tara. I knew he was a junkie, and I suspected Serena had acquired the habit too. I threatened to make it public in court, and she caved in.'

'But why?'

'Because she couldn't afford that.' His voice was grim. 'The head of the studio had a son who died through his cocaine addiction, and he's violently anti-drugs. I hoped it might have brought her to her senses, but I soon realised I was wrong.'

Phoebe gasped. 'You mean she's an addict?'

'Oh, yes.' His voice was almost matter-of-fact. 'The signs were all there. I knew she'd dabbled in the old days—she even had a supplier in sleepy old Midburton—but now it's serious. She has to have treatment.'

He gave her a quizzical look. 'Now you understand her violent reaction when you called her the Snow Queen.'

He drew a deep breath. 'Last night was sheer hell. I'd already contacted a specialist who runs an excellent clinic near London. He came down at once with an ambulance, and persuaded Serena to go with him. She was in a bad way—apparently her supplier had let her down—and she agreed.'

'Oh, God,' Phoebe said with anguish. 'Poor Tara.'

'She only knows that Mummy is ill, and has to be

made better. I think she'd already sensed that something was very wrong. I felt such a bastard getting rid of you like that, but I had no choice. I couldn't tell you what was going on until I'd got Serena herself to admit she had a problem. I didn't know how long it would take, and I had to make sure you were safe.'

'I understand,' she said gently. She hesitated. 'Dominic, I think I know who her supplier is. There's a perfume shop in the precinct where I got the dolls' house. She used to go there regularly.'

He sighed. 'I suppose I'd better put the local drugs squad onto it. Naturally Serena wouldn't give them away, although she was pretty frank about a number of other things. It was she who got Tony to come down here and spy out the lie of the land, and he tipped her off about you. The last thing she wanted was for me to establish another relationship.'

'So she really did want you back,' Phoebe said quietly.

'No,' he said, 'she wanted Tara. And while I had custody she couldn't have her. Another of her lovers is a producer, and he's planning a new version of *Alice in Wonderland* with a mix of actors and animation. Serena had decided Tara should play Alice.'

He paused. 'She's blown her own career, but she could survive if she made Tara a star, earning big money. Once she'd secured my cooperation, either in or out of marriage, she was going to take her to California.'

He shook his head. 'Do you know, at one point she almost had me fooled? I really began to think she'd come back just for Tara. Because she loved her and wanted to be a mother to her. And I hated myself, because that was the last thing I wanted.'

'Why?'

He looked at her, the grey eyes tender. 'Because I was in love with you, and I knew that Serena would never stand competition—even for a man she didn't want. I was worried that she'd see how I felt, so I kept away from you, even though it nearly killed me after that evening we spent together. Then Tara made me kiss you, and I was lost. And Serena knew it. She's been like an unexploded bomb ever since.'

'And she's really gone—to this clinic?'

'She didn't have a choice. If she's cured, she's still got a life. And she'll be able to see Tara too. But Tara will live with us.'

He paused. 'Or am I taking too much for granted? I came here to ask you to marry me, but perhaps you don't want me. I couldn't blame you. One way or another, I've led you a hell of a dance since we first met.'

Phoebe reached up and kissed him. 'Then I shall have to get my revenge,' she whispered. 'By leading you one hell of a dance too. When we're married.'

He said her name, his voice breaking, and held her and kissed her as if he would never let her go, and they were both laughing and both crying, and it was their own special Christmas miracle.

'Let's go home,' he said at last. 'Your presents are under the tree, and there's one excited little girl who can't wait to see you. And one demented dog.'

'How did you get in here, anyway?' Phoebe asked belatedly.

'I saw Lynn and her parents round the corner,' he explained. 'Lynn gave me a hard lecture, and also the spare key. I've to post it through the letter box when we leave.'

Phoebe hesitated. 'Dominic—it will be all right—with Tara? She wanted—you and Serena...'

'It won't all be plain sailing,' he said. 'And we're crazy if we think differently. But she told me to ask if she could be a bridesmaid, so I think we have her consent. And she made me bring this, too.'

He took a small box from his pocket. Phoebe gasped when she saw the exquisite ruby flanked with diamonds.

'Oh, Dominic. It—it's beautiful.'

'You see? I was even prepared to try bribery to get you.' He put it on her finger and kissed her hand.

'I don't need bribing.' Phoebe put her arms round him, enfolding him with her love, because his need was as great as hers.

She smiled up into his eyes. 'I have a far better reason than that for marrying you.'

He rested his cheek on her hair. 'And what's that?'

'Why,' said Phoebe, 'I'm doing it just for Tara.'

MILLS & BOON

Next Month's Romances

Each month you can choose from a wide variety of romance novels from Mills & Boon. Below are the new titles to look out for next month from the Presents™ and Enchanted™ series.

Presents™

Dishonourable Intent	Anne Mather
The Reluctant Fiancée	Jacqueline Baird
Marriage on the Rebound	Michelle Reid
The Divorcee Said Yes!	Sandra Marton
Wildcat Wife	Lindsay Armstrong
The Secret Mother	Lee Wilikinson
That Kind of Man	Sharon Kendrick
Wild and Willing!	Kim Lawrence

Enchanted™

The Fortunes of Francesca	Betty Neels
Shotgun Marriage	Day Leclaire
Holding on to Alex	Margaret Way
Bride By Day	Rebecca Winters
Wife for Real	Jennifer Taylor
Marriage Bait	Eva Rutland
Wild Horses!	Ruth Jean Dale
Help Wanted: Daddy	Carolyn Greene

Available from WH Smith, John Menzies, Volume One, Forbuoys, Martins, Tesco, Asda, and other paperback stockists.

MILLS & BOON

Celebrate the most romantic day of the year with a delicious collection of short stories...

VALENTINE DELIGHTS

A matchmaking shop owner dispenses sinful desserts, mouth-watering chocolates...and advice to the lovelorn, in this collection of three delightfully romantic stories by Meryl Sawyer, Kate Hoffmann and Gina Wilkins.

Plus FREE chocolate for every reader!
see book for details

Available: January 1998

Available from WH Smith, John Menzies, Volume One, Forbuoys, Martins, Tesco, Asda and other paperback stockists.

WINTER WARMERS

How would you like to win a year's supply of Mills & Boon® books? Well you can and they're FREE! Simply complete the competition below and send it to us by 30th June 1998. The first five correct entries picked after the closing date will each win a year's subscription to the Mills & Boon series of their choice. What could be easier?

THERMAL SOCKS	RAINCOAT	RADIATOR
TIGHTS	WOOLY HAT	CARDIGAN
BLANKET	SCARF	LOG FIRE
WELLINGTONS	GLOVES	JUMPER

T	H	E	R	M	A	L	S	O	C	K	S
I	Q	S	R	E	P	M	U	J	I	N	O
G	A	S	T	I	S	N	O	I	O	E	E
H	T	G	R	A	D	I	A	T	O	R	L
T	A	C	A	R	D	I	G	A	N	A	T
S	H	F	G	O	L	N	Q	S	W	I	E
J	Y	H	J	K	I	Y	R	C	A	N	K
H	L	F	N	L	W	E	T	A	N	C	N
B	O	V	L	O	G	F	I	R	E	O	A
D	O	E	A	D	F	G	J	F	K	A	L
C	W	A	E	G	L	O	V	E	S	T	B

C7L

Please turn over for details of how to enter ⇨

HOW TO ENTER

There is a list of twelve items overleaf all of which are used to keep you warm and dry when it's cold and wet. Each of these items, is hidden somewhere in the grid for you to find. They may appear forwards, backwards or diagonally. As you find each one, draw a line through it. When you have found all twelve, don't forget to fill in the coupon below, pop this page into an envelope and post it today—you don't even need a stamp! Hurry competition ends 30th June 1998.

Mills & Boon Winter Warmers Competition
FREEPOST CN81, Croydon, Surrey, CR9 3WZ
EIRE readers send competition to PO Box 4546, Dublin 24.

Please tick the series you would like to receive
if you are one of the lucky winners

Presents™ ❑ Enchanted™ ❑ Medical Romance™ ❑
Historical Romance™ ❑ Temptation® ❑

Are you a Reader Service™ Subscriber?   Yes ❑   No ❑

Mrs/Ms/Miss/Mr........................Initials ....
(BLOCK CAPITALS PLEASE)

Surname ....

Address ....

....

....Postcode ....

(I am over 18 years of age)

C7L

One application per household. Competition open to residents of the UK and Ireland only. You may be mailed with offers from other reputable companies as a result of this application. If you would prefer not to receive such offers, please tick box. ❑

Mills & Boon® is a registered trademark of
Harlequin Mills & Boon Limited.